GREEN SPRING UNIVERSITY

Schooling The
QUARTERBACK
GSU BOOK ONE

LAURA JOHN

Cover Designer: Brittany Franks with Chaotic Creatives

Editor: Swish Design and Editing

Sensitivity Reader: J.P Jackson

To Pat.
You might not read romance, but you sure know a lot about football.
Thanks for making sure I don't ruin this book.

CHAPTER ONE

WHAT IS the big deal about sports?

It's a question I've been asking myself for twenty-two years. Actually, I probably wasn't forming coherent thoughts like that as an infant, but I'm sure by the time I was three, I was already confused by people's obsession. So, I've been going over it for at least eighteen years and still don't understand.

Green Spring University lives and breathes sports, *all* sports, so it's not even a seasonal thing, which sucks. If it wasn't for the fact that they have one of the best law schools in the country, I wouldn't be attending. GSU is also in the same city as my nana, an added bonus I love.

Staying close to Nana has been more of a blessing than I thought. I knew starting university at sixteen would be a challenge, but I wasn't prepared for how lonely it would be. If I was across the country from the only person in my family who has always loved me unconditionally, I don't know what I'd do.

I'm not the most social person in the world, but having at least one friend is nice. I didn't have anyone when I started here. My two best friends weren't as *gifted* as I was and couldn't accelerate their learning. Graduating two years early isn't an easy feat. I felt like a baby when we said goodbye because I cried so much. The only reason I let the tears fall was because my father wasn't around. My friends were always my safe space, and I was a sixteen-year-old about to go off on my own for the first time. Of course, I was nervous and upset and needed a minute to let my feelings out. If my father had seen me, he would have screamed at me for behavior like that. In his eyes, men don't cry.

That way of thinking is, of course, what's wrong with our society. Anyone can cry and feel their feelings. It's healthier than keeping it all bottled up. But I was a good child and kept my feelings inside around my family like I was taught.

When I arrived in Green Spring, my nana welcomed me with open arms. She was kind and warm like I always remembered her growing up, making me wish I could have visited her more as a child. My parents never showed me love like she did. At first, I thought it was because parents and grandparents show love differently, but I quickly found out it was because my parents were just plain old assholes.

I came out to Nana about six months after moving here, and she told me she loved me no matter what. I knew my parents wouldn't react well, but with the safety of distance and with Nana's love and support, I decided to come out to them as well. My mother cried, my father yelled, and they told me I wasn't welcome in their house anymore. I haven't spoken to them since. Nana, of course, tore my parents a new one and told them if I was no longer welcome, neither was she and cut off all contact with them.

With Nana's constant positivity, I never gave up hope of finding new friends, and even though it took a few years, I eventually found a group of people I clicked with who also didn't understand everyone's obsession with sports. Most of us are athletically challenged, except for Sasha, who is a geek but also a dancer. Thankfully, he isn't a geeky jock. There's no way we'd get along as well as we do if he was, or maybe I'm being judgmental.

Sports people are all the same.

The *only* thing they seem to care about is... sports.

I'm currently studying in the main area of the campus center, which isn't my usual preference, but I'm waiting on my new tutoring student, and this is where he wanted to meet.

Three young women dressed in Kelly green and black with white sneakers and tiny koala temporary tattoos on their cheeks giggle as they pass by my table. The women are talking about the soccer game tonight, and I can't help but shake my head. I just don't understand it. Nothing about any sport thrills me, even after extensive research and trying to see the appeal.

"Are you Gabe?" a man asks in a deep voice.

I put on my professional smile and look up from my textbook. I was not expecting my newest tutoring student to be a drop-dead gorgeous giant, but he is. The man standing in front of me has to be at least six foot four with thick brown, chin-length hair, broad shoulders, and forest-green eyes. How on earth is it possible for such a handsome man to exist?

I'm an *extremely* intelligent person, but this man's perfect body has me second-guessing if magic is real. Maybe a spell was put on him when he was a baby to bless him with such good looks.

Giving my head a shake, I stand and reach my hand out toward the man. "I'm *Gabriel*," I reply, emphasizing my full name, as I hate it when people shorten it. "Are you Chase?"

His face lights up, and he nods. Holy cow, he even has a perfect smile—all straight teeth and pearly white too. How was he gifted with such beauty?

"That's me, but I also go by Ando if you want to use that instead," he offers.

I blink at him a few times. Why would I call him *Ando* if his name is Chase?

"Chase is fine by me..." I assure him after an awkward pause. "In your email, you said you were struggling with your business law and ethics course?" I ask, wanting to confirm.

His perfect smile drops, making my stomach churn a little, which I'm not used to. *Am I getting sick?* That doesn't feel right. I think my stomach is hurting because of the loss of Chase's smile. I don't like him looking upset. I want to bring his happy demeanor back, which again is weird because I don't know this guy.

Why should I care so much that he's bummed about his grades? I've had other tutoring students look just as upset, if not more, and I didn't have this kind of gut reaction, wanting to bring their smiles back.

Chase answers my question before I can dwell too much on these odd feelings. "Yeah, the legal jargon just isn't clicking. I can't flunk this course and risk bringing my GPA down. I have to keep it up, or I won't be able to play. This is my last year, and I want to bring home the championship win. I won't be able to do that if I'm benched for flunking my classes," he tells me, his dark brows pulling together and causing worry lines on his forehead.

An unusual desire to smooth them out courses through my veins. What the hell is wrong with me?

"We're over halfway through this semester, and it's still not clicking. I need help. My grades are on the fence right now."

I push away the new feelings again because now is not the time to dissect them. I can do that when I'm alone. Right now, this student needs my help. This man has my brain a jumbled mess. Never before have I had such a problem focusing on the task at hand.

I became a tutor because I hate seeing anyone struggle with their grades. And as much as I don't get sports, I understand how important they are to those who love them.

"I'll do my best to help you," I assure him, meaning the

words more than ever. "I've got a pretty decent track record with other students I have helped."

His smile returns at my words, lighting up his entire face and easing the knot sitting rock solid in the bottom of my stomach. "I've heard awesome reviews. That's why I reached out. You helped a buddy of mine last year. He said he wouldn't have passed if it wasn't for your help."

My cheeks heat at the praise. I've never been good at taking compliments.

A group of rowdy people wearing more green and black passes by us, stopping to give Chase high-fives and congratulating him on his last game. I patiently wait for them to move on while mentally planning where to move us. This location isn't going to work for a study session.

"Would you be okay with heading to the library?" I check after the crowd moves on.

"Sure," Chase agrees with a shrug and an easy grin.

I tip my head, pack up my stuff, and start walking to the campus library. Chase follows beside me, waving and saying hi to people as we go.

How does he know so many people? I guess that's what happens when you're a popular jock.

"What's your major?" Chase asks as we make our way.

"I already completed my Bachelor of Arts majoring in Sociology. I'm in my second year of law school now," I explain, keeping my focus ahead, not turning to look at him like most people probably would. I don't need his good looks distracting me.

Chase gasps, gaining my attention. His eyes are preposterously wide, and his steps falter momentarily. "How is that possible? You look like you're nineteen." He blinks at me a couple of times, probably trying to figure out what's going on.

"I'm twenty-two," I inform him. "I started college when I was sixteen. Finished my bachelor's degree when I was nineteen and will hopefully graduate from law school when I'm twenty-three."

Chase's brows shoot up even more, and he shakes his head. "So, you're like genius-level smart?" he inquires.

I lift a shoulder, not loving the term *genius*. "I'm smarter than the average person my age."

"You're a hell of a lot smarter than I am," Chase murmurs.

"Our difference in levels of intelligence doesn't matter," I assure him. "And I highly doubt that you're dumb. You're just stuck. It happens to more students than you could imagine."

"Thanks, but sometimes I have a hard time believing that," he replies, shoving his hands in his pockets. For the first time since I met him, he appears self-conscious.

This isn't the same man whose chest was puffed out as he high-fived his fellow students. This is a person who has a serious amount of doubt.

I've seen people like this before, but I've never wanted so badly to solve all their problems for them as I do with Chase. I want to be the person who helps him get rid of his insecurities. To show him he's capable of anything.

Helping with his studies shouldn't be hard for me, but dealing with these new emotions might.

CHAPTER TWO

WHO WOULD HAVE THOUGHT that my new tutor was a genius? Mattias did *not* tell me that when he recommended Gabe. He also didn't mention how cute he is.

Gabe is a lot shorter than most of the guys I hang out with. If I had to take a guess, I'd say he's only five foot ten, but his height suits him. He's slim with a head full of thick, curly, dirty blond hair and plush, naturally pink lips. However, the focal point of his face isn't his kissable lips. It's his giant glasses. He's got that nerd-chic look down pat, and I find it extremely attractive, which is new for me. The guys I normally hook up with are jocks.

Another thing that really threw me off when I met him was the lack of recognition when he looked at me. Being the star quarterback for the GSU Koalas means most people at least know my face, but Gabe was completely unphased, something I'm not used to.

"So, you've been at GSU for six years now?" I check as we approach the library.

When we arrive, I hold the door open for Gabe. He gives me a weird look before going inside. *Is it not normal for people to hold doors open for others?* My mom raised me with manners and would slap me upside the head if I didn't use them.

"Yes," he replies, making his way into the library. I follow behind, easily keeping up with him. One of the perks of having long legs.

"And you don't know who I am?" I question when we arrive at a table.

"You're Chase Anderson," he replies with my full name, which I included in my email earlier this week.

"Yeah, but do you know *who* I am?" I try again as we both sit down.

Gabe blows out a breath and moves his glasses up to pinch the bridge of his nose.

"If you're trying to hint at who you are in the sports world, no, I don't know who you are," he tells me. "I don't watch sports." I gasp, which makes the hot nerd roll his eyes. "I hate to break it to you, Chase, but not everyone's world revolves around sports. Some people have better things to do with their time."

I stare at him like he's grown a second head. I knew there were people out there who didn't like sports, but I've never met one before. It's like I'm sitting next to an alien right now.

"Have you ever been to a game?" I inquire.

Gabe sighs. "Yes, I have, and I've watched a lot of different sports on TV. I spent most of my childhood being forced to watch them, and it never clicked with me."

My mind is being blown right now. I understand being confused by sports until you've been to a live game, but normally, that changes things for people. You feed off the crowd's energy, and there is nothing like it. At least nothing I've ever experienced.

"But that's enough talk about sports," Gabe insists in a business-like voice. "We are here to help you pass this class. Now, let's see what you're struggling with the most. Did you bring your recent papers and tests like I requested?"

I smack my forehead and shake my head. I knew I was forgetting something, but the day has been kind of crazy. It completely slipped my mind. "Sorry," I reply, keeping my head down.

Gabe blows out his breath. When I look back at him, he's pinching the bridge of his nose again, and his plush lips are slightly pursed. Why do I find that kind of hot?

What would it feel like to have those lips wrapped around my cock?

Internally, I give myself a shake to stop thinking about my tutor sexually. I reach into my backpack to pull out my textbook, hoping that will be enough for now. "I'm struggling with everything," I tell him, handing him the book. "I know it's important to learn about legal stuff when it comes to businesses, but every time I read about terms, I instantly forget them. Everything is going in one ear and out the other."

Gabe hums in understanding while flipping through the pages. "You need a way to connect with the legal terms," he states, keeping his eyes on the pages as he talks. "What kinds of things are you into?"

"Sports," I reply with a charming smile, not that Gabe sees it since his nose is still in the book.

He sighs but tips his chin. "Give me a couple of days to devise a plan." He closes the book and finally meets my gaze again as he hands it back to me. His soulful chestnut eyes are mesmerizing, making me forget that we're talking about my educational future for a second. "I'll also print off a few old exams so that we can assess your knowledge."

I nod, pulling my attention back to this moment. His idea feels like it's as good of a plan as any. I don't have a clue how he'll have me connecting with the information, though. We're over two months into this semester, and each day, I feel dumber and dumber.

"You're going to have to put in an extreme amount of effort to get your grade up," Gabe tells me with a serious look on his cute face. "Are you willing to give up any partying you're currently doing and put in the work?"

"Anything to save my ass," I assure him. I don't bother adding I'm already a dedicated student and rarely party.

He hums his acceptance of my answer. "Email me your current schedule and any known changes from now to the end of the semester. When we meet next, I'll have an updated schedule for you, including specific study times. I'll meet with you at least twice a week to start. We can up that to more if necessary."

I pull out my phone and do as he tells me, knowing I'll forget if I wait until I return to my apartment.

"Sent," I tell him with my best smile, which doesn't seem to affect him at all. He honestly looks bored, which again confuses me.

"I'll email you once I've come up with your plan," he says, standing and grabbing his backpack.

"Do you think texting would be easier?" I ask, grabbing a piece of paper and a pencil from my bag. Then, writing down my number, I hand the paper to my new tutor. "I'm kind of shit for checking my email, but I'll always respond if you text me."

He takes the paper and nods with that emotionless look on his face. "Fine. I'll text you in a few days." With those words, he leaves, and I'm left in a weird state.

Gabe is like no one I've ever met. Even though I hired him to help me with my grades, I find myself wanting to know more about him, which is another new thing for me. I've never been the guy who wants to go deeper with people. Most of my friendships are surface level, and *all* my hookups are *just* sex. Yet Gabe has me wanting to peel back his layers and find out what makes him tick. To figure out how to make him smile and bring joy to his face

CHAPTER THREE

Gabriel

TWO OF MY ROOMMATES, Max and Victor, are playing chess on the coffee table when I get home after my meeting with Chase. Our other roommate, Sasha, is playing on his computer in the corner of the living room.

When I first arrived at GSU, I lived on campus, not wanting to be completely reliant on my nana but quickly tired of the campus lifestyle. Thankfully, I met Max at the end of my second year, and he was looking for a new roommate. Fortunately, Max owns this place and doesn't charge much for rent. He doesn't even have a mortgage since his uncle left it to him. He learned right away that he hated living alone. Now, he shares the space with Victor, Sasha, and me. Our rent keeps him from working, which is great for him. Not so much for me. I work myself to the bone to make ends meet.

Without any parental backing, I have to plan for everything.

In addition to tutoring, I worked at a coffee shop until I was old enough to bartend. Now, I work at a pub a couple of blocks away a few nights a week.

"How was your tutoring session?" Victor asks while I hang up my coat.

November evenings in Michigan can bite, and the month has only just begun. Heaven knows it's only going to get worse as the season progresses. You'd think, having lived in this state my whole life, I'd be used to winter by now, but it's highly unlikely that I'll ever truly be comfortable with it.

I shrug. "Not bad. Nothing I can't manage. I just have to figure out how to help a jock connect with legal terms. Any suggestions?"

"Does he have a secret love for Dungeons and Dragons?" Max inquires with a smirk.

"Not that I'm aware of," I reply.

"Then I've got nothing."

I chuckle and flop onto the couch, watching them continue their game.

"I could ask Carter," Sasha says, mentioning the basketball player he's been giving dance lessons to for the last month.

"That might be helpful if Chase plays basketball, but I don't actually know what sport he plays," I admit.

"That would have been a good question to ask him," Sasha replies with a smirk.

"Yeah, how did that not come up while you were meeting?" Victor adds.

"I don't know. You know how I am with sports. I would be completely content if they didn't exist. It was obvious he was a jock from the way he carried himself to how he knew so many people. I just didn't think to ask what sport he played."

"You should probably start there," Max suggests.

Chase sent me his schedule, so I open the email, praying it tells me what sport he plays. I don't want him to think I'm a jerk for not asking when we met. And if I have to send him a text, it's going to come across that way.

"What college sport primarily plays games on Saturdays?" I ask.

When I look up from my phone, all the guys stare at me like I'm an anomaly. Right, none of them are sports guys. That's why we're friends.

Looking back at my phone, I google my question, and

football is the first answer. With that information, I head to the GSU football website and search the roster. Chase's picture pops up right away, and I find out he's the quarterback. Apparently, he's really talented too. At least, that's what the article I click on tells me.

"Did you figure it out?" Victor asks.

"Yup," I reply, without looking up from my phone. My focus is on the article and the picture of Chase in the middle of a football field. "He's a football player."

"I'm no help there," Max voices.

"We're no help on *any* sport," Victor adds.

"I watched a lot of football growing up," I tell them. "Maybe when I do some research, things will click into place."

"That's a lot of effort for a tutoring student," Sasha points out, sounding suspicious of me.

"Not really. I've done similar things for others before," I counter. "Remember that one guy who I related everything to *Mario Kart* for?"

"Yeah, but you *like Mario Kart*," Victor reminds me.

"Oh, he's hot," Sasha says, handing his phone to Max, who lets out a whistle and then gives it to Victor.

"*Now* things make sense," Victor voices.

I sigh. "It has nothing to do with how attractive he is," I argue. "You should have seen how upset he was. Any of you would do the same."

Max tilts his head from side to side. "I wouldn't have agreed to double my workload to help someone *just* because they were upset. But I might have if there was the chance of some *extra* extra-curricular activities." He waggles his brows suggestively. "If you catch my drift."

I push my glasses up and rub my eyes. I'm never going to hear the end of this. But if they think, for one second, I'm going to admit I agreed to put in a *lot* of extra work just because Chase is hot as sin and stirs new emotions in me, they've got another thing coming.

"Okay, I'm going to my room now," I tell them, making my way up the stairs.

"Remember to be quiet if you're going to jerk off to pictures of the quarterback," Sasha teases, making the others laugh.

I flip them the bird like the mature person I am and walk to my room. I *wasn't* planning on jerking off, but now that Sasha has planted the seed, my chubbing cock wants to play.

Stupid roommates. They're lucky I love them like brothers.

When I get to my room, I close the door behind me and flop on my bed, pulling out my laptop so I can research the shit out of football.

My friends are right. I wouldn't put this much effort in for just anyone, but I'll never admit it to them. Besides, I don't know my true motivations for accepting Chase as a tutoring student. Maybe it's the feelings he's stirring inside me, but honestly, that should have me wanting to do the opposite. It should have me bolting, but I can't make myself do that. I'm obviously attracted to him, but it's how my heart beats a little faster for him, and the way it physically hurts me to see him upset is really throwing me for a loop.

Besides, just because I'm into him doesn't mean he'll feel the same way for me. And that's not me bashing my looks. I know I'm not ugly, but not everyone is into nerdy guys. Besides, I don't even know if Chase is gay.

GSU is one of the most supportive schools out there of the 2SLGBTQIA+ community, and I'm aware there are openly gay people on our sports teams because it's something that is talked about a lot around campus. But as someone who pays zero attention to sports, I wouldn't know if Chase is one of them.

My alarm blares on my phone, which is directly beside my head, causing me to startle.

Shit. I fell asleep researching football and trying to relate legal terms to sports analogies. Thankfully, my class this morning is one I don't have to study hard for. If I'm being honest, *most* of my classes are that way, but that doesn't mean I allow myself to slack off.

Last night was a rarity for me, which should have me second-guessing my decision to help Chase. What will happen next if I'm already putting off my regular studying for him? Nothing. That's what's going to happen next because I'm in charge of myself. I just have to budget my time better. Last night was a one-off, that's all.

I straighten my glasses on my face and stretch my limbs, forcing myself out of bed. After I'm dressed, I pack my bag for the day and stumble down the stairs to where I know a pot of coffee is waiting for me. Thank all things good for auto-mated coffee machines.

The heavenly aroma of the nectar of the gods wafts into my nose as I enter the kitchen, making my mouth water. I pop a piece of bread into the toaster before pouring myself a cup, doctoring it to my liking.

"Next year, I'm not taking any morning classes," Sasha murmurs, entering the kitchen looking as tired as I feel.

I chuckle and reach into the cupboard for a second cup.

"I'm fine with mornings once I've had the glorious bean juice," I reply, pouring his coffee and handing it to him.

"It does make mornings easier, but I still stand by my decision to stop taking morning classes," he tells me, taking the cup and inhaling the sweet smell.

"Are we still on for board games tonight?" I check, and

my toast pops up. I move to butter it while waiting for his response.

"Shit," he grumbles. "Sorry, I forgot to tell you that Carter needs an extra dance lesson. I couldn't tell him no. You should see those sweet puppy dog eyes he uses on me. That child knows his hidden talents and uses them against me. Thank the heavens he's only eighteen, and I don't date babies, or I'd be in even more trouble."

It's funny that Sasha sees an eighteen-year-old as a baby, considering he's only twenty-two, but I get it. Carter is just starting his college career, and Sasha is nearing the end of his.

From someone as full of life and into dance as Sasha is, you wouldn't think he'd be in school to be a lawyer like I am, but he is. He's going to be a damn good one too.

Laughing, I wave him off. "It's not a big deal. I'll just use the spare time to figure out more about football and how to relate it to business legal terms."

"You're really pulling out all the stops for this guy," Sasha notes.

I shrug and take a big bite of my toast, not wanting to respond.

If my friends didn't know me so well, I'd say they were blowing this out of proportion, but I've dropped tutoring students for less in the past. So I understand their fascination with my response to Chase.

Once I finish breakfast, I say goodbye to Sasha and make my way to campus, grateful we live close by so I can walk. With my warm jacket zipped up tight, I make the short trek, thankful it isn't snowing today, not that I would let that stop me. Michigan winters can be unpredictable, and I've walked through it all.

As I walk, I call my nana like I do most mornings.

"Good morning, Gabriel. I was wondering if you were going to call this morning," she answers, and I chuckle.

"Sorry I didn't call yesterday," I apologize. "It started out a mess and ended oddly. I fell asleep studying."

"Tell me about it," she encourages.

I blow out a breath. "The morning was just one of those days. It was like everything was working against me. I forgot to set my alarm, burned my toast, and was almost late for my first class," I explain.

"Those happen, but I'm sorry you had to go through that," she empathizes. "And what was odd about the ending?"

"I have a new tutoring student. I agreed to help him even though it's going to take a *lot* of extra effort on my end," I tell her honestly like I always am with her. Nana and I don't keep secrets, and I don't plan on changing that now.

"Is it going to affect your studies?" she asks.

I ponder the question for a moment before shaking my head, even though she can't see me. "It shouldn't, but it's unusual for me to agree to extra work to help someone I don't know."

"You have some reasons to agree. He is paying you," she reminds me.

I hum in response because she isn't wrong. "Yes, he is paying me, but I've turned down other students before who were also willing to pay me. So why did I agree this time?"

"I'd love to answer that question for you, but I'm afraid you're the only one who can," she replies softly.

"I know. I'm sure I'll figure it out. Maybe I'm turning over a new leaf and am becoming more sympathetic to others."

Nana giggles. "Maybe, but there is probably another answer. Let me know when you find out."

"I will," I assure her. "What are your plans today?"

"I was thinking about visiting Doris. She started a new puzzle the other day and invited me to join her."

I smile, loving that Nana has some amazing friends. After my family kicked me out and Nana cut off contact, I felt guilty that she didn't have them in her life anymore, but she has a much better 'chosen family' now. Thankfully, the people she surrounds herself with are fantastic and more loving than those we are related to by blood.

"That sounds like a great day," I reply. "I should let you go so you can get ready. I'll see you on Sunday for dinner."

"I can't wait. Have a good day. Love you," she tells me, and I can hear the smile in her voice.

I'm so grateful I have Nana in my life. She truly is one of the best people around.

CHAPTER FOUR

Chase

THE ROAR of the crowd is so loud it's almost deafening, and the smile on my face is so wide I bet the people at the top of the bleachers can see it clearly. Our team just won, and the ecstatic energy on the field right now is what I live for.

"That's how you fucking do it, boys," Brett Henderson, better known as Hendo, the team's tight end, shouts, ramming his body into mine, giving me some sort of celebratory bro hug.

"We slaughtered 'em," Callan Abel, who goes by Abby, one of our wide receivers, calls out, joining us to celebrate our win.

The rest of the team meets us on the field to join in on our mini victory party before we head to the locker room to have our after-game meeting with everyone.

"Great game, boys," Coach Donnelly says. A bunch of us are sitting next to each other and high-five, fist-bump, and playfully shove shoulders. "But don't think this win gives you a free pass to slack this week. Take your day off tomorrow, like you've earned, but I better see all your asses in the training room bright and early Monday morning. We've been doing great this season, and we are well on track to bring home the championship trophy this year, but that won't be possible if we get cocky. So, celebrate your win tonight, enjoy yourselves, then give me your all on Monday and the rest of the week."

"Yes, Coach," we all reply loudly before heading to the showers.

I love playing for GSU. There isn't any other school I would want to attend. Their stance on being a safe place for the 2SLGBTQIA+ community is one of the main reasons. When they first started implementing rules against the orientation-based unspoken policies that have governed sports for too long, hoping to better support their gay players and help change the toxic parts of sports culture, there was some push-back. But as time moved on and the school refused to back down, the homophobes were weeded out and eventually stopped coming to this school. Now people are aware that if you want to play for GSU, you can't be a dick. Everyone on the sports teams actually signs a contract acknowledging that they agree with the school's beliefs. If any bigotry is found, they will be immediately removed from their team and face disciplinary action. GSU takes pride in being a school for *everyone*.

I've been out and proud since I was ten, but it hasn't always been easy. I wasn't easy to beat up due to my size, even as a kid, but it didn't stop the hurtful words from cutting deep. If they weren't picking on me for being gay, they were calling me stupid.

Kids can be assholes. I'm glad GSU doesn't stand for any of that. Just last year, a star hockey player was expelled for harassing another student. The school stands firm in its beliefs and doesn't look the other way for *anyone*.

"Coming to Abby's place?" Hendo checks with me once we are both dressed and I'm packing my bag.

I shake my head. "I need to focus on getting my grades up," I tell him honestly. "My tutor is meeting with me in the morning to go over his plan for me. I don't want to be dead on my feet."

Hendo nods, knowing how important this is. If I don't get my grades up, I'll be benched, which would affect everyone. "It sucks you can't come to celebrate, but I understand. I'm gonna crash at Abby's after the party. I'll see you tomorrow."

I wave at him and a few other teammates as I head out. Making my way to my car, I scroll on my phone to see how my best friend, Rio, did in his soccer game. My smile grows even wider when I see his team also won tonight. With an extra joyous heart, I head to the apartment I share with Hendo and Rio.

"Congratulations on your win," Rio tells me when I walk through the door.

"You too, bro," I say, pulling him in for a brotherly hug and patting his back. I've always been a touchy kind of guy, and thankfully, Rio doesn't mind. "I heard that you won the game for your team."

Rio's cheeks are pink when I pull back. He's never taken praise easily.

"It was a team effort, but I did score the winning goal," he tells me with a smirk.

I tap his shoulder with my fist. "That's my boy."

He chuckles, rolling his eyes at me. "Stop buttering me up like that, or I'll get a big ego."

"Impossible," I reply, then head for my door to drop my stuff off, not wanting to be the sloppy roommate who leaves his shit wherever he wants.

"I have to head to bed early tonight, but did you want to watch a show or something before I crash?" I ask when I'm back in the living room, where Rio is now lounging on the couch. He's typing away on his phone with a deep frown. I hate how upset he looks, but he puts on a fake smile when he looks up at me.

"Sure, a show sounds good," he responds, and his tone tells me he's trying to hide something.

"Did you have other plans?" I inquire.

He sighs but shakes his head. "I did, but it turns out they just got canceled."

"Sorry, man. Want to talk about it?"

"Nah, I want to forget about it," he says, and I let him drop it for now.

Rio has always been the guy who needs to think things through before he talks about it. When he needs me, he'll open up. So, I don't push him to do something he isn't ready for and turn the television on, ready to distract him with some dumb show.

My alarm blares bright and early, and instead of cussing under my breath like I do most mornings, I kick off my blankets with a smile. Why am I so excited to get out of bed this morning? It can't possibly be to study for a class that is making me feel like a dumbass. There is a strong possibility it has to do with the world's cutest tutor. I'm not sure why I'm so drawn to him, but I don't feel like overthinking it right now.

With an extra pep in my step, I change into some clean clothes, make myself breakfast, and go over the schedule Gabe sent me last night. Not much is changing on my end except meeting with him twice a week and more targeted study sessions. What kind of schedule does Gabe have that he's able to fit me in so easily? Most students at GSU have part-time jobs, and he has other tutoring students, yet he didn't push back on any of my currently scheduled activities. Maybe he understands it would be hard for me to change most things.

Hendo walks through the door as I finish my scrambled eggs, looking exhausted. "Why are you home so early?" I question, taking my plate to the sink to wash, dry, and put away.

"Abby and his girlfriend got in a fight at the ass crack of dawn," he supplies. "Since I was awake, I wasn't waiting around to find out how it ended."

I chuckle, and my phone dings, reminding me I need to meet Gabe in thirty minutes.

"Who's got you smiling like that?" he asks, and I look around, wondering who he's talking to because I'm not smiling that much, am I? "I'm talking to you, Bozo," he adds.

Shit, I do have a dopy look on my face.

"Just excited to get my life back on track, is all," I explain with a shrug.

"Suuure…" Hendo draws out, obviously not buying my excuse. "And the sky is pink."

"It's blue," I reply, my brows pulling together.

Hendo shakes his head with a big grin. "It's a figure of speech. I'm calling you out on your bullshit. There is no way you're *that* happy to study."

"Fine, the tutor is cute, but what's wrong with having some positive motivation to get to a study session?" I check.

"You gonna ask him out?" he asks.

I tip my head from side to side. "Maybe, but he doesn't like sports, so I doubt he'll say yes."

Hendo gasps. "He doesn't like sports? Is he an alien?"

I laugh, loving that my friend is thinking exactly like I am.

"I guess not. Did you know there are other things that matter besides sports?" I question, using Gabe's words from the other day.

My teammate shakes his head. "Impossible. We've just got to convert this guy. It could be fun." The smirk on his face is almost evil, but I like the way he thinks.

"Let me get a read on him first. I don't need him dropping me because I won't stop talking about sports."

Hendo presses his lips together but eventually nods.

"Well, if you need any help getting this guy to like sports, let me know."

"Will do," I reply, and my phone dings again. "Shit, I've got to go. Gabe doesn't strike me as the kind of guy who likes people being late."

Hendo waves at me, heading to his room as I grab my bag and head out the door.

Time to figure out if Gabe has come up with a plan to get my grades back up and understand this damn class.

CHAPTER FIVE

CHASE WALKS through the coffee shop's doors two minutes before ten. His entire face lights up when his eyes land on me, which sends tingles crawling up my arms and down my spine. Why am I reacting like this? I'm sure he smiles that brightly at everyone.

"Mornin'," he says with a toothy grin, dropping his bag on the floor and pulling out the chair across from mine.

"Good morning," I reply. "Did you get my text with the updates to your schedule?"

He tips his head while digging through his bag. "I sure did. It looks great to me. I also remembered to bring the stuff I was supposed to last time."

I take the papers and offer him a smile, which only results in his growing larger. I didn't know that was possible. How is someone so radiant and happy? Maybe I'm just a cynical person. "Thanks. Why don't you grab a coffee? Then we'll start on my plan," I tell him, reaching into my bag to grab my notes.

While he's placing his order, I spend a moment taking him in again. He's wearing a pair of gray sweats that should be illegal for how they make his ass look and a GSU Koala hoodie. When he walks back, it's going to take everything I have not to let my gaze drop to what has to be an impressive package. His hair is messy like he didn't put any effort into it, and maybe he didn't. Either way, it still looks good on him. I wish I had the ability to roll out of bed and look good, but I would scare small children if I didn't tame my curls.

"So, what's the game plan?" Chase asks when he gets back with a black coffee. I didn't know people our age drank black coffee. "Something wrong?" he checks, obviously noticing the way I'm studying his coffee.

I shake my head. "No, I just haven't seen anyone drink a black coffee that isn't like my dad's age."

Chase chuckles, the sound deep and inviting, making more tingles erupt beneath the surface of my skin. "It's not so much a preference as it is an avoidance of unnecessary calories," he supplies. "The athletic team trainer has us on some serious meal plans. Drinking plain black coffee is an easy way to get more things I enjoy in my diet, especially with the way I enjoy my caffeine."

So he's a caffeine addict like me, but what college student isn't?

"That makes sense," I reply, handing him a practice test. "Would you mind taking this for me so we can obtain a baseline of how much you're struggling?"

His beautiful smile drops, causing that annoying knot to form inside me like the first time we met. That's something I need to figure out how to stop.

Chase takes a deep breath as his eyes zero in on the piece of paper in my hand, but he eventually takes it. "I guess that's a good idea," he mumbles.

He's quiet as he works his way through the test. I should be spending this time going over his previous tests and assignments, but I keep casting glances at the jock. Even with his brows pulled together and a pencil in his mouth, he's still attractive.

He taps on the table when he's thinking hard about a question. As I figured, the ones giving him the hardest time are about terminology. When he's finished, I compare his answers to the answer sheet.

"So, how badly did I fail?" he checks when I've finished.

I set the paper down before looking into his gorgeous eyes. They are almost pleading for me to give him an answer he'll appreciate. It's evident in this moment that I can't fail him.

"This wasn't about pass or fail. It's about getting a base-line," I remind him. "Just like you told me when we met, the terms are throwing you for a loop. I bet they are even making you second-guess other stuff you know."

He runs a hand through his dark brown hair, somehow making it look even better as he does it. "I think you're right, but I don't know how to gain a better grasp on this."

"That's why you hired me," I explain with an even smile.

Chase stares at me for a moment, almost like he's studying *me*, but his grin finally comes back. "So, what's the plan?"

I hand him the paper I've been working on the past few nights. "Think of this like your cheat sheet," I tell him. "I've written down every major term from your class and found a football term to relate to it."

His brows shoot up, and when he looks at me this time, it's with an awe-filled expression. "This is fucking brilliant," he whispers.

I shake my head as my cheeks heat, probably turning the brightest shade of pink. "It was nothing," I argue. "We'll still have to go over them often to make sure they stick, but I'm hoping by changing your outlook that eventually things will click."

His smile is back to the bright and vibrant one he had on his face when he first walked through the doors of the coffee shop. It makes my heart beat a little faster and eases the pit in my stomach. There has to be a way to permanently keep his smile in place.

We spend the next hour going over what his professor

currently has him working on and how he can use his new cheat sheet to help him with the project.

"I thought you didn't like sports," Chase says when it's time for us to pack up.

"I don't," I confirm, shoving a few things in my bag.

"Then how did you manage to pull this off," he asks, holding the paper I gave him.

"A lot of research," I tell him honestly.

"And you did that for me?" His dark, thick brows pull together, obviously not understanding why. But *I* don't even know why, so I can't give him that answer.

"You are paying me," I remind him.

"Yeah, but I'm not paying you that much. This had to have been a lot of work," he counters.

I shrug. "It was no biggie," I lie.

He stares intently into my eyes for a few seconds. It feels like he's looking into my soul, which is why I glance away and fiddle with my bag.

"Maybe you're secretly a sports lover," Chase offers.

I shake my head. "I most definitely am not."

"Come to the hockey game with me tonight," he adds.

I look up at him, wondering if this is a joke, but he looks serious. "Why would I do that?"

"Because I asked?" he checks, sounding hopeful.

"I can't," I tell him, even though a part of me wants to say yes, which is weird as hell.

Why would I want to go to a hockey game with the football team's quarterback? Sports people confuse me, and I know absolutely nothing about hockey except that it's played on ice and the players wear skates.

"Why can't you?" he asks, not dropping it.

"I have dinner with my nana every Sunday," I reply, even though I don't owe him an explanation.

"The game doesn't start until seven. What time do you

have dinner? I could pick you up after you're done," he offers.

"Why do you want to take me?" *What's his motive?*

"Because I have a goal to convert you into a sports lover," he tells me with a cocky grin. I'm sure that smile has worked on a lot of people in the past, but I don't want it working on me. "And I think you're super cute, so a date with you wouldn't be a hardship at all."

I freeze.

Wait… date?

He thinks I'm cute?

What the hell is happening?

"Please don't turn me down," he pleads with an adorable pout and the most perfect puppy dog eyes. How the hell am I supposed to say no when he looks like that? "I mean, unless you're not gay and my gaydar is way off, then by all means, correct me, and I'll shut my mouth."

"Your gaydar isn't off," I mumble. "But why me? I'm sure you have your pick of people to go out with." I make sure not to mention gender since I don't want to assume that he's gay just because he's asking me out. He could be bi.

"You're smart, and you intrigue me. I don't want anyone else right now. I want you," he replies, causing my heart to race a mile a minute.

I'm into Chase, or I wouldn't be putting in the extra effort for him, but I'm apprehensive about dating him. What would we even have in common? I don't do casual flings, but dating a guy like Chase seems like a recipe for disaster. Even hanging out as friends could be dangerous territory. I need to keep my walls up.

"I can't tonight," I repeat.

His smile slips for a second, but it's quickly back with a cocky tilt to it this time.

"Not tonight doesn't mean not forever," he replies,

reading between the lines. "I'll just have to keep asking until you say yes." With those words, he heads out the door, leaving me dumbfounded.

Is he really going to keep asking me until I say yes?

What happens when I do?

CHAPTER SIX

THE APARTMENT IS quiet when I return from my meeting with Gabe, which doesn't surprise me. Hendo is most likely still sleeping after being up late last night, and I bet Rio is out for a run. I don't know how he does it *every day*. Don't get me wrong, I love a good run, but I'm more of a treadmill kind of guy in the winter.

I hang up my coat, then head into the living room, plopping down on the couch to do a little studying before the hockey game tonight. It's been a tradition for Rio, Hendo, and me to hit up as many hockey games as possible. Considering we are all athletes, it's not possible to attend *every* game, but we do our best. Not only to show the team our support but also to cheer on another good friend of ours, Ben Cooper, better known as Coop. He's the goalie and has been killing it this season. I wouldn't be surprised if they win the championship this year.

After I'm comfortable on the couch, I pull out Gabe's cheat sheet and study it with a smile. It's still blowing my mind that he came up with this for me. It must have taken him *hours*, if not days, to create this. Why would he put that kind of effort into it? If he hadn't shot me down, I would have considered maybe he liked me, but that's doubtful now.

I give my head a shake because, honestly, it doesn't

matter. What matters is I have a tool at my fingertips that will hopefully help me pass this class.

My thoughts drift to Gabe while I study, and I consider reaching out, even though I'm not struggling as badly as I normally do. I kind of just want to talk to him, but that might be weird, so I push down the desire, keeping my focus on my work.

I'm not sure how long I've been studying when the door swings open, and Rio appears, dripping in sweat but with a contented grin.

"Good run?" I check.

He nods. "You should come with me sometime," he encourages, knowing full well what my answer will be.

"Hard pass until the weather warms up. I'll run on the treadmill tomorrow."

He chuckles, kicks off his runners, and disappears into his room, emerging a moment later with a change of clothes in his arms.

"Are we still on for the game tonight?" he asks, leaning against the wall.

I nod. "Coop would kill us if we missed tonight. Our appearance has become a lucky ritual for him. I don't want to be the one to jinx the team when they are on a hot streak."

Rio chuckles, but all of us sports guys are the same with our superstitions.

"Perfect. Want to grab dinner beforehand?"

"Sounds good to me," I reply. "I'll wake Hendo while you shower."

He tips his head in acknowledgment, then heads into the bathroom.

Stretching my arms above my head, I push myself up and make my way to the kitchen for a few ice cubes. Nothing says rise and shine like a brisk wake-up.

With the ice in my hand, I head to Hendo's room, opening the door as quietly as possible. My lips twitch to find him passed out *solid*. You'd think a stupid prank like this would get old, but it never does. An enthusiastic energy races through my veins while I tiptoe across the floor. Once I'm at the edge of his bed, I carefully peel back his blankets, lift his boxers, and drop the ice cubes inside. With lightning speed, I bolt out of his room. His screams echo off the walls and sound more like a teenage girl than a twenty-year-old guy. I narrowly miss the pillow he throws at me, but that doesn't stop my roaring laughter as he calls me every name under the sun. Moments like this never cease to bring a smile to my face, but I will definitely have to watch my back for the next couple of days. Payback is a bitch but worth it.

"Now that you're awake, Rio and I were wondering if you wanted to grab a bite to eat before the hockey game," I inquire from the doorway.

Hendo sighs dramatically but eventually mumbles an agreement, so I leave him to get dressed.

It's going to take my roommates a little while to get ready, so I settle on the couch again, picking my studying back up. There is a small bit of hope that pushes the dread I had for this course out of my chest. Fingers crossed, I'll finally get the hang of things and pass the class with the bare minimum grade I need.

"What's with the intense face?" Hendo asks before sitting beside me.

"Just trying to study with this new guide my tutor made me," I reply, showing him the sheet Gabe created.

"Damn," Hendo mutters. "This must have taken some serious effort. Didn't you say he wasn't a sports guy?"

"He isn't. Apparently, he just did a lot of research."

Hendo gives me a skeptical look. "Are you sucking his dick already?"

I choke out a laugh and shake my head. "Nah, man, it's not like that. And believe me, I would know. I invited him to the game tonight, but he told me no."

It's Hendo's turn to laugh. "That must be a first for you."

"It is," I admit begrudgingly.

"Then why did the guy make that sheet for you?" he questions. "Are you paying him a shit ton of money?"

"Not more than what most people charge," I tell him.

He hums in acknowledgment but still looks confused.

"I think he's just a nice guy," I say after a moment.

Hendo lifts a shoulder. "Or… he's into you."

"If he was into me, why wouldn't he agree to come to the game tonight?" I counter. Obviously, he had other plans, but if he wanted me, you'd think he would have offered to come another time.

"Because he's not a sports guy," he reminds me. "Maybe you have to find something he likes first, *then* invite him to a game."

I ponder his suggestion for a minute, then Rio comes out of the bathroom.

"I'm starved. Are we ready to go?" he asks.

Hendo and I nod, then we all move to get our coats on before heading out to one of our favorite restaurants.

Dinner is quick and filled with chatter about sports and the usual stuff. As soon as our bill is paid, we make our way to the arena, ready to cheer our friends on.

"How's the new tutor?" Rio asks as we head into the arena.

The air is chilly, but the energy radiating off the crowd makes it bearable. The only thing that would make tonight better would be if a certain sexy nerd was by my side. I've never had to chase after someone before. It's both intriguing and frustrating at the same time.

"It's going good, I think. He created a sheet comparing legal terms to football terms. It might actually work to make things stick in my brain."

He lets out a low whistle. "Someone is already getting some serious special treatment, huh? You told me he wasn't a sports guy. That couldn't have been a quick and simple thing."

"That's what I said," Hendo buts in. "I think the tutor has a thing for our guy here."

"That's undecided at the moment," I murmur.

"Do you like him?" Rio inquires.

I tilt my head from side to side. "He's cute, but I don't really know him."

"But you'd like to," Hendo goads.

"Yeah, I would," I whisper. "I invited him out tonight, but he turned me down," I explain to Rio, catching him up.

"Wow, how is your ego after a hit like that?" he teases.

"A little bruised," I reply, rubbing my chest as if I'm actually injured. "But I'm not giving up so easily. I've decided I'm going to keep asking him out until he says yes."

Rio chuckles. "Good luck with that."

"You know me, I'm always up for a challenge. Who knows, maybe Hendo is right, and he *does* like me."

"Why do you want this guy anyway?" Rio inquires. "You come from two different worlds. Are you actually wanting to date him or just fuck him?"

I ponder his question for a moment, trying to come up with an answer, but it never comes. Why *do* I want Gabe? I mean, he's sexy and intriguing, and I'd love to find out if his cheeks turn that gorgeous shade of pink when he comes. But is that all I want? I don't think so, but that leads to Rio's second point. Gabe and I come from two different worlds. How would that even work? Maybe that's why he didn't want to come tonight.

"I don't actually have an answer to your questions," I mumble, and Rio shrugs.

"That's fine. Just make sure you come up with one eventually."

I nod, and the crowd cheers as the teams come out for the national anthem.

I'm not sure how I'm going to come up with the answers, but the one thing I do know is I want to get to know Gabe better. And if we just so happen to fall into bed together, that wouldn't be a bad thing, either.

The hockey game goes by in a blur of cheering, shouting, and some banging on the glass. Before I know it, the Koalas have won, and we are waving at Coop as he leaves the ice to head to the locker room. We spend a little while talking with fellow students sitting near us, then head back to our apartment.

When my head hits the pillow, all I can think about is the only person ever to shoot me down.

I'll see the sexy nerd in a few days. Besides studying to show him that I'm not an idiot, I also want to come up with a way to turn his no into a yes.

CHAPTER SEVEN

THE LIBRARY IS BUSY TONIGHT. Low, murmured voices fill the space while I search for an empty table for Chase and me to study. Eventually, I find one near the back and drop my bag onto it, pulling out a chair and sitting down.

> Me: The library is busy tonight. I found a table near the back on the second floor.

> Chase: *thumbs up emoji* OMW

I push my phone to the side and study for my classes to pass the time until he gets here.

" 'Sup, tutor?" Chase asks, pulling me out of my little world and startling me.

I clench my book a little tighter before plastering on my friendly, professional smile. "Are you ready to study?"

He beams at me, showing off his perfectly white teeth before pulling out the chair across from me. "As ready as I'll ever be."

"Is the cheat sheet helping?" I check.

He nods. "This thing is a lifesaver. I don't know how I'll ever repay you for coming up with it."

The tips of my ears and cheeks go hot, and I wave him off. "Don't worry about it. I want to make sure you succeed. I'd do it for any of my tutoring students," I lie, the words slipping off my tongue with ease.

He stares at me as if evaluating if I'm telling the truth. To my relief, he doesn't push the envelope because I don't know what I would say if he called me out. His forest-green eyes hold mine for a beat longer than what would be considered normal, and I slowly get lost in them.

I clear my throat to bring myself back to the present. "Okay, let's test how things are coming along."

"Let's do it," he replies with a determined expression etched on his handsome face, a complete contrast to when we first started.

I pull out a list of questions I prepared and start the session.

By the time we finish, I'm pleasantly surprised that Chase is already getting the hang of things. He still has a long way to go, but he's improved a hell of a lot in just three days.

"You must have been doing a lot of studying on your own," I muse out loud, my eyes zeroing in on the way his cheeks pinken just the slightest bit.

Chase grabs the back of his neck and lifts a shoulder. "I might have been doing a little more than normal for me. I wanted to impress you," he confesses, catching me off guard. "But also, with the sheet you made for me, it has made things a lot easier, and I've actually *wanted* to study."

I can't help but smile at his words, loving that I was able to help him already. "I'm glad things are clicking for you," I say quietly, bashfulness briefly taking over me.

"It's all thanks to you," he tells me, his voice soft and comforting. "What are you up to tonight?"

His random question catches me off guard, and I struggle to respond. "Studying," I answer once I'm able to gather my thoughts.

"Would you like to grab a bite to eat with me?" he inquires.

I nibble on my lower lip, stunned that he's asking me out again.

"Why?" I reply instead of giving him a yes or no answer.

"I realized that maybe inviting you to a hockey game for a first date was a bit too much. So maybe a late-night bite to eat where we can learn more about each other would be better."

I mull over his words, unsure how to respond. "I don't see how our dating would work," I whisper. "We are polar opposites. There is no way we have anything in common."

"Why don't we hang out and put your theory to the test?" he suggests. "Come hang out with me for a bit and meet the side of me that isn't a jock. Maybe we'll have more in common than you realize."

I should say no. Go home and study. But there is a part of me that wants to find out if we really do have something in common.

Just as I'm about to tell him yes, my phone vibrates. My blood runs cold as I read the message.

Victor: Max just got rushed to the hospital.

"I have to go," I tell Chase, grabbing my stuff as fast as humanly possible and running out of the library.

I hear Chase call my name behind me, but I don't stop until I arrive at the parking lot, where I text Victor to find out where Max is.

Me: Which hospital?

"What's going on," Chase asks when he catches up to me.

"One of my best friends and roommate is in the hospital," I tell him, feeling like my chest is going to burst from how hard my heart is beating. I've never felt fear like this in my entire life.

Max isn't one to go to the doctor on a good day. I can't even begin to wonder what happened if he was forced to go. Worry creeps up my body and squeezes my chest like a vice grip, making it hard to breathe. Why the fuck is this happening?

As soon as Victor tells me which hospital, I pull up my rideshare app, but Chase grabs my arm, stopping me.

"Let me drive you," he offers.

I shake my head quickly. The offer is sweet, but I won't be able to give Max my total concentration with Chase around.

"I appreciate the offer, but I don't know how late we'll be there, and he doesn't know you. I know Max better than most people, and he isn't going to want strangers to see him in a vulnerable state," I tell Chase, turning my focus back to my phone to find a rideshare. Thankfully, there is one only two minutes away. I hit the button to book the ride and wait for them to arrive.

Chase shoves his hands into his pockets. It's obvious by how he's worrying his bottom lip and furrowed brows that he wants to argue, but he doesn't. Instead, he offers, "If you need anything, let me know. Okay?"

I tip my chin in acknowledgment, not sure what to say.

Chase stays by my side in awkward silence until my ride shows up. His presence is oddly comforting, but I don't want to think too much about it. When the car arrives, I give him a small wave before getting in, praying that traffic isn't bad tonight.

The streetlights and headlights from other vehicles pass by in a blur as the driver takes me to the hospital. I try to keep my thoughts positive, but the silence from Victor is almost deafening.

Why isn't he updating me on Max's condition?

As soon as the driver pulls up to the front doors, I rush out, making a beeline for the administration desk. Before I get there, Victor catches my attention and waves me over.

"Where is Max?" I question frantically. "Is he okay? What happened?"

My heart is racing so fast now, making me dizzy. Am I going to pass out? Victor must sense that I'm on the verge of hitting the floor and guides me to sit in a chair.

"He's in the room with the doctor. He had a severe allergic reaction to something he ate and went into anaphylactic shock," he tells me. "They say he'll be okay, but I've never seen anything so scary." He fiddles with his hands while staring at the floor. His face is white, and his bottom lip looks raw like he's been chewing or sucking on it for a while.

"I didn't know Max had allergies like that," I murmur.

"No one did," he replies. "He was just as shocked as I was when his face blew up like a balloon. Then his tongue started to swell. Obviously, he didn't have an EpiPen, so I called 9-1-1 and prayed they would arrive in time."

I grab Victor's hand when tears start to well in his eyes. I feel for my friend. I can only imagine how terrified both of them must have been.

"Thankfully, someone else at the restaurant had an EpiPen. They helped Max out until the paramedics arrived. They told me that the EpiPen probably saved his life."

I can't help but gasp. We could have lost our friend tonight, and the thought makes my stomach churn.

My head is spinning when a young woman in bright pink scrubs stops in front of us.

"Normally, we wouldn't let you back because you're not family, but Max wants to see you, and since you're his room-mate, I'm going to let it slide for tonight," she tells Victor. "I'm bending the rules, so make it quick. Your friend needs to rest."

"Can I go too?" I request.

She smiles at me and lifts a shoulder. "I don't see why not, but like I said, you need to make the visit short. We're keeping your friend overnight to make sure he doesn't go back into anaphylactic shock and to monitor his vitals. Hope-fully, all goes well, and you can take him home in the morning."

We nod and follow her to Max's room.

"What are you doing here?" he asks me, then shoots Victor a glare.

"Don't give me that look," Victor grumbles. "I thought you were going to die and panicked. I would have called Sasha, too, but we all know he doesn't answer his phone when he's at the studio. I'll fill him in in the morning."

Max's face softens, and he nods. "Fine," he mutters.

"How are you feeling?" I inquire.

"A little loopy and very tired," he replies, his eyelids drooping as he talks, like he's struggling to keep them open.

"I'm happy you're alive," Victor whispers.

"Me too," Max says. "I've never experienced anything like that. I'm going to have allergy testing done soon to find out exactly what I'm allergic to so I can avoid it at all costs. I don't ever want to go through that again."

"The nurse said we can't stay long, but if you need anything, text me, and I'll be here as soon as I can," Victor assures our friend.

"Thanks, I appreciate you being there for me." The

moment the words are out, his eyelids droop again, so I pat him on the arm.

"Get some rest. We'll pick you up in the morning," I tell him before walking out with Victor.

Neither of us says anything as we walk down the hallway until I randomly blurt out, "Chase asked me out again."

Victor's eyes go wide. "What did you say this time?"

"I didn't have a chance to say anything," I tell him. "I was about to when you sent me that text."

"Well, shit," he mutters. "Didn't mean to cockblock you."

I chuckle, feeling lighter now that we know Max is most likely going to be fine. "It was probably for the best. I'm still not sure *why* he's interested in me."

"It's because you're hot," he plainly says as if he's telling me the grass is green.

I scoff. I mean, I'm not *ugly*, but I wouldn't consider myself hot, either.

Victor shakes his head with a smirk on his lips. "You don't see it, do you?"

"What's there to see?" I counter. "Even if *you* think I'm hot, I'm not hot enough to date a jock."

We walk through the front doors of the hospital, and Victor stops moving. "First of all, looks aren't everything," he tells me firmly. "Second of all, maybe he's being genuine when he asks you out. But none of that matters in the end. What really matters is, do you want to date him?"

I mull over his question while he books us a rideshare—something we probably should have done *before* standing outside in the cold.

We wait in silence, but no matter how hard I think about Victor's question, I can't come up with an answer. Do I want to date Chase? Maybe... but I'm scared. I fall easily for people. I don't want a broken heart. Obviously, I'll play it off like nothing happened—I've gotten good at that—but I hate feeling like shit because I let my heart run away from me.

I've figured out ways to keep my feelings under control, but I can tell already that letting Chase in will knock down all the walls I've carefully built for myself.

Am I ready for that to happen?

CHAPTER EIGHT

Chase

IT'S BEEN three days since I've seen Gabe. Each of those days, I've typed out a text to ask how he's doing before swiftly deleting it. I don't want to come across as weird, but I've been worried for him. I also want to know how his friend is doing, but we don't have that kind of relationship. We aren't dating. We aren't even friends, at least not yet. We are just a student and his tutor, so asking him personal questions feels out of line.

Even on the ridiculously long bus ride for our away game, I couldn't stop thinking about Gabe. Borderline obsessing about someone is *not* like me at all. I did, however, manage to finish some homework.

It makes me happy that things no longer feel like they are in a completely different language. I know I still have a long road ahead of me to get my grades up from where they are teetering on the fence, but I finally have faith that I'll be able to do it now.

Today is game day, and even though I still can't stop thinking about Gabe, I won't let that stop me from playing my ass off and doing my best.

"Ready to kill it, boys?" Hendo shouts in the locker room as we're getting ready.

A round of cheers and shouts of agreement ring out, which brings a smile to my face.

Coach Donnelly gathers us for our pregame chat as soon as everyone is good to go. The energy in the room is charged. We are four weeks away from the end of the regular season, but if we keep things up, we'll be on our way to the playoffs —something GSU hasn't been able to pull off in over five years.

Last year, we were ridiculously close but got knocked out in the second round. We don't want a repeat of that this year. We want to bring home the championship win, but we'll only do that if we keep our heads in the game and give it our all.

As we head out to the field, my only focus is football. It's like the rest of the world fades away. It's always been this way for me. I love it. That's why I've always said football is my calling. No matter what is going on in my life, nothing else matters when I step on the field.

The national anthem plays, and our team stands on the sideline with our hands on our hearts, but the second it's over, we all share a look that says, '*It's time to wipe the field with this team.*'

Hometown advantage is a thing, and even though the majority of the fans in the stands are rooting against us, we aren't going to let that hold us back. We came here to win, and that's what we intend to do.

"That's fucking right, boys!" I yell when the game ends, and we've won by three points.

A bunch of us slap each other on the backs and give bro hugs while we celebrate our win, then head to the locker rooms to clean up and prepare for a long-ass drive home through the night.

A permanent smile is on my lips as I head to my changing area. It gets even bigger when I see a text from my best friend congratulating me on our win. Rio didn't have a game tonight as his final soccer game of the regular season was last night, which they won. The championship bracket will be announced on Monday, but the Koalas are already in good rankings. We just have to keep our fingers crossed that they make it all the way to the end and bring home the trophy this year. It would be really fucking awesome if both my best friend and I were championship winners this year.

While on my phone, I check to see how Coop and the hockey team are doing. It always sucks when they are playing a game the same night we are, but for some reason, as long as we're playing or it's an away game, us not being there doesn't matter. But the superstition is still there.

The boys and I once missed a home hockey game we could have been at, and the team lost horribly. We won't make the same mistake again. Or it's more like Coop won't *let* that happen again. Tonight's hockey game is still on, but the Koalas are in a killer lead. I fist bump the air before taking a much-needed shower.

My muscles are sore as fuck when I change into some comfortable clothing for the bus ride home. I should hit the athletic building tomorrow for a massage or at least a hot soak in a jacuzzi. Since there isn't a hockey game tomorrow, the only thing I have to work around is my tutoring session. I'd also like to ask Gabe out again, but there is a thin line between being determined and charming and being desperate and creepy. I really don't want to cross that line.

The thing is, I don't know how to pursue someone. Normally, if I ask a guy out, they say yes. I'm finding myself in unknown territory. It's both scary and exciting at the same time.

Maybe I'll be able to devise a plan on our drive home. There's even a chance my teammates might be able to help me out.

After I'm changed and have my bag packed, I make my

way to the bus, where I find Hendo leaning against the side, talking with a few of our teammates.

"Ready for the long-ass drive home?" he asks after I've thrown my bag under the bus.

I shrug. "I guess so. Sure would be nice if they could figure out teleportation, though."

He chuckles and nods. "That would be the life."

Everyone is exhausted as we slump into our seats, but there's no rest for the college athlete, and most of us pull out a textbook or a laptop to study before we stop for dinner.

"You look right enthralled there," Hendo notes while I work on a project my professor gave the class. "I take it the tutoring is helping?"

I nod with a smile. "Gabe is the best tutor I've ever had."

"Are you going to ask him out again?" he checks.

I shrug and close my notebook. "I'm not sure, man. I *want* to, but I don't want to come across too strong and scare him off. The worst thing that could happen would be him dropping me."

"And you don't think asking him out every time you see him is too strong?"

I chuckle. "That's my dilemma."

Hendo purses his lips like he's deep in thought. "It's weird seeing this side of you," he states. "Why this guy? Why not any of the hundreds of guys who would willingly throw themselves at your feet."

"I don't know," I reply quietly. "There's just something about him, and maybe I'm getting tired of the easy targets."

"I wish you nothing but the best as long as this doesn't affect your game."

I laugh and shake my head. "Nothing could affect my game. You know how much football means to me."

"You eat, sleep, and breathe the sport," he says with an easy smile.

"Damn right. Now, are you going to help me come up with a plan to convince my hot tutor to go out with me?"

Hendo chuckles and lifts his shoulder. "Sure, why the hell not."

CHAPTER NINE

IT HAS BEEN the craziest couple of days, but Max is doing well. He was released from the hospital the morning after his attack and hasn't shown signs of any new allergic reaction, which is fantastic. That doesn't mean we have been able to relax around him, though. I've even made Victor and Sasha text me while I'm working at the bar with updates, just in case.

We're all sitting in the living room studying together, and of course, Victor, Sasha, and I keep casting glances at Max to make sure he's okay. Not much should change in a couple of minutes, but from how quickly Max went into anaphylactic shock the last time, anything is possible.

"That's enough!" Max shouts randomly, snapping his textbook closed and causing us to jump.

"What's wrong?" Victor asks, his brows pulled together.

"All of you are walking on pins and needles around me, and I'm sick of it. I'm not going to randomly drop dead, so stop acting like it," he scolds us.

"We just care about you," Sasha tells our roommate, who's still glaring at us.

Max sighs, throwing his head back against the couch. "I understand that, but it's been four days since the reaction, and I'm *fine*. I understand the concern, but I promise everything has been good since I've been home… no hives, no itchy skin, nothing. I just want us to go back to how we were before."

"It's kind of hard to do that when you see one of your best friends almost die," Victor mumbles.

"I think it will be easier for us to relax once you get your allergy testing done," I supply.

Max presses his lips together, obviously mulling over my words, and finally, he nods. "Fine, but can you at least *try* to become better actors so your fretting isn't so obvious?"

I chuckle, Victor nods, but Sasha scoffs. "I'm an amazing actor."

"Normally, yes, but in this situation, not so much," Max replies, making Sasha roll his eyes.

My phone buzzes in my pocket while the two bicker. Shit, I lost track of time and need to leave now.

I stand and head to the coat closet to grab my backpack and jacket.

"Date with the hot jock?" Max asks, obviously trying to pull the attention away from himself.

"It's a tutoring session," I sass.

"But it could turn into something more if you only say yes," Victor adds.

I pinch the bridge of my nose, causing my glasses to push into my forehead a little. "Why are you all so set on me saying yes? I think out of anyone, you all would see why dating a jock is a mistake."

"Not all jocks are bad guys," Sasha states. "Just like not all nerds are nice guys. Why are you judging him before you even know him?"

"What exactly are we going to have in common?" I argue.

"You won't know until you get to know him," Max says.

I sigh but don't reply. What exactly is there to say? So, I put on my jacket, hat, and gloves and head out the door.

"Good luck with your date," Sasha shouts as I leave. Even

though I hate how pushy they are being, it still brings a smile to my lips.

The walk to the coffee shop is chilly but gives me time to think. Is Chase going to ask me out again? If he does, what am I going to say? Should I say no again or listen to my friends and give him a chance?

By the time I arrive, I still don't have answers to any of my questions, but there isn't time to dwell on them right now. I need to put on my tutoring hat and set my focus on the subject at hand.

I'm surprised to find Chase already here, even though I'm fifteen minutes early. He waves at me with that killer smile, making my lips turn upward.

"I got you a coffee," he says when I drop my bag and pull out the chair across from him.

I stare at the drink. It's the exact same thing I always order, but how did Chase know that? We've only had coffee once, and I got mine before he arrived. He didn't ask what I was drinking the last time we were here, and I highly doubt he would have been able to guess it from just looking at it.

"I asked the barista what you normally order," Chase answers my unasked question with a smirk and a tinge of pink on his cheeks.

Looking across the café, my eyes land on Stefanie at the counter, helping another customer. We used to work together before I got the job at the bar, so it makes sense that she was able to tell Chase my go-to order.

A warm, fuzzy feeling flutters through me at Chase's kindness. Even though he's made it obvious he's interested in me, I still wasn't expecting a thoughtful gesture like this. Maybe I was wrong to write him off as a dumb, full-of-himself jock. Actions always speak louder than words, and he's showing me the kind of guy he really is.

"Thanks," I whisper, taking a sip of the sweetness.

"Any time," he responds, sounding genuine.

I'm not sure what to say next, so I dig into my bag, ready to start our session.

We review the assignment Chase is currently working on, and I answer all of his questions. I've always loved helping the students I tutor gain a better grasp on their classes, but I enjoy it even more with Chase. When his face lights up, and he understands the concept better, it fills my chest with pride.

"Are you having dinner with your nana again tonight?" Chase asks when we're finished, and I nod.

"Every Sunday," I tell him, a little shocked he remembered.

"Would you like to hang out after?" he inquires with hope-filled eyes. "My friend bought me tickets for this Christmas light display thing that's supposed to be really cool."

"Isn't it a little early for Christmas activities?" I reply. "Thanksgiving hasn't even happened yet."

Chase chuckles. "I thought the same thing, but apparently, it's super popular, so they set up the display at the beginning of November and run it until the middle of January to allow people to check it out."

I don't immediately reply, just stare at him, trying to figure out if I actually want to say yes.

"Do I have something on my face," Chase checks, wiping his hand over his face.

I can't help but smile. "No," I assure him, shaking my head. "I'm just thinking."

"You seem like the kind of guy who does that a lot. Why don't you step out of your head this one time and accept my offer? Let's spend time getting to know each other. We don't even have to call it a date. It could just be two friends hanging out," he offers, making it much harder to say no.

I take a deep breath and tip my chin. "Okay," I whisper. "We can go... *as friends*."

Chase fist bumps the air and lets out an excited cheer, drawing the attention of a few people in the café.

"You're not going to regret saying yes," he promises while he packs his bag. "Text me your nana's address, and I'll pick you up at seven."

With those words, he rushes out of the café, not giving me a chance to change my mind.

What the hell did I just agree to?

CHAPTER TEN

MY PALMS ARE a bit sweaty as I walk up the path to a cute little house that I guess belongs to Gabe's nana. It's a warm brown with little pink flower boxes under each window. I wonder what they look like when filled with blooming flowers in the spring and summer.

We said this wasn't a date, but that doesn't stop my nerves from getting the best of me. Maybe because I don't plan on letting him keep me in the friend zone for long. He's convinced himself that we're from two different worlds, and we kind of are, but maybe we have more in common than he thinks. Neither of us will find out until we get to know each other better. I just need to convince him to open up to the idea.

With a shaky fist, I raise my hand and knock on the door, pleasantly surprised when I'm immediately greeted by the cute nerd who has all my attention right now.

"You came to the door?" he whisper shouts through his teeth.

"Was I not supposed to?" I ask, looking around. *Why is he talking so quietly?*

"Who is it?" a woman calls out.

"Just my ride, Nana," he shouts back, pushing me out the door. "I'll call you tomorrow."

"Gabriel Joshua Miller, are you planning on leaving

without a hug," she scolds him, her voice getting louder like she's getting closer.

Gabe pushes up his glasses and pinches the bridge of his nose while blowing out a breath. "You stay right there," he demands, pointing his finger at me before turning and walking around the corner.

"I love you, and I'll call you tomorrow," Gabe says to who I'm assuming is his nana, his voice barely loud enough for me to make out the words.

"I love you, too, but I expect to meet your *ride* the next time he picks you up," she replies, her voice louder. Did she deliberately raise it so I could make out the words clearer?

"Bye, Nana," he says, and a second later, he finally makes his reappearance. With a tight grip on my arm, he pulls me back down the path toward my car. "Why did you come to the door?" he questions, ushering me farther away from the house. Once we are a decent distance from the house, he lets go of my arm, and I immediately miss his touch.

"Isn't that what people do?" I reply, confused by his attitude and harsh tone.

"Only if it's a date," he tells me. "If you're just picking up a friend, most people send a text instead of coming to the door."

His brows are pulled together, lips pursed, and arms crossed against his chest while he rushes to my car. Is it weird that even when angry, I still find Gabe hot?

"Sorry," I apologize, even though I'm still not sure I'm in the wrong. "My mom raised me not to be a jerk who honks his horn or sends a text. But if it bothers you, I will next time."

Gabe blinks at me as if he can't find his words. "Thanks," he murmurs.

Pulling the fob out of my pocket, I unlock the car. Something inside me is dying to open the passenger door for Gabe, but another part, a smarter part, is saying that will only piss him off more. So, I force my feet to keep walking to the other side of the car.

"Have you ever been to this light show?" I check with Gabe once he's buckled, then shift the car into drive.

"I've honestly never even heard of it," he replies. "But I looked it up after our meeting. It looks amazing."

I nod. "It's supposed to be magical. I know this isn't a date, but if we get stuck under some mistletoe tonight, I'm going to have to kiss you."

I cast a quick glance at him, and his cheeks are pink.

"I've heard it's bad luck not to," he tells me quietly. "And I wouldn't want to bring that on you, so I guess I'll take one for the team if the situation arrives."

Is Gabe actually flirting with me right now? I've never seen this side of him, and I'm dying to see more.

"You're a noble man," I tease, and he chuckles.

The light show is on the outskirts of town and takes us about an hour to get there, which isn't ideal for a Sunday night, but I'm willing to break my routine a little for a chance to spend more time with Gabe.

Once we arrive, I find a parking spot, and we make our way to the event space, which is taking place in a giant field. It reminds me a little of going to a corn maze.

At the entrance, we are handed a pamphlet with directions highlighting everything that's set up. The first place we walk through is designed to feel like an old-time town with Christmas lights *everywhere.* There are makeshift storefronts with tables in front for people selling various holiday-themed items. Food trucks are parked to the side for those who are hungry, and at the end of everything is Santa's Village. It was smart of them to arrange it like that, so everyone has to walk through the vendors *before* getting a picture with Santa.

I'm sure they'll sell a lot more things that way.

"This really *is* magical," Gabe notes as we take our time strolling through.

"I can't wait to see the Tunnel of Lights," I tell him.

He nods. "That's what caught my attention the most when scrolling through their website."

We stop at a few booths, and I make a mental note to try to come back to buy a few things I see Gabe eyeing.

"Are you from Michigan?" I inquire as we make our way to the Tunnel of Lights.

He looks at me with a soft smile. "Yup, born and raised. What about you?"

"Same," I reply. "I grew up about an hour away from Green Spring. My parents didn't want me moving too far from home, and I always had my sights set on GSU."

"It's nice to be close to family," he supplies. "I'm not sure if I could have made it without Nana. But maybe that's because I was still a kid when I started college."

"What about your parents? Do they live close?"

Gabe presses his lips together and shrugs. "They live on the other side of Michigan, but even if they did live close, I wouldn't see them. They stopped talking to me the day I left my hometown."

My brows shoot up and my feet falter. "Why would they stop talking to you?"

I don't understand how a parent could cut off contact with their child. My mom calls me at least once a week and texts almost daily. What would it be like to go *years* without hearing her voice?

"They are homophobic," he supplies. "When I came out, they disowned me. At first, it was mind-boggling how fast it all happened, but after a while, I realized it shouldn't have come as a surprise. I wasn't the kind of son my dad wanted. He was just looking for the right excuse to finally get rid of me. My sexuality was the breaking point."

My blood boils, and my fingernails bite into my palms as I make a tight fist. I don't anger easily, but who the fuck disowns their kid for something they can't control? I'm obviously aware it happens, but in this day and age, things are getting better. Unfortunately, there are still backward thinkers. If I ever have the displeasure of meeting Gabe's father, I'm going to punch him in the face.

"I'm sorry you went through that," I say.

Gabe lifts a shoulder, not looking as upset as I feel. "I've had time to process it, and I'm over it. It's honestly for the best that they shunned me. Looking back now, I realize that my dad was emotionally abusive, and my mom was just neglectful. I'm better off without them in my life. Besides, I have Nana, and she's the best person."

I'm glad he has *someone* in his life who loves him for him.

"This is amazing," Gabe murmurs in an awe-filled manner when we enter the light tunnel. His eyes are big, taking in the amazing display. While I should also be checking out the lights, I can't seem to take my eyes off the adorable man beside me.

We continue to walk, and occasionally, I brush the back of my hand against his, playing it off as an accident when, in reality, I'm just dying to touch him. Even though we are both wearing gloves, and I'd love to touch his skin even more, this is the next best thing.

When we reach the end, we are greeted by some reindeer in a pen in front of Santa's Village.

"Do you think we can pet them?" I ask Gabe, itching to touch the animals in front of me.

"I don't think so," Gabe tells me, killing my joy by pointing to a stupid sign that clearly instructs us to keep our hands to ourselves since the reindeer might bite.

I narrow my eyes at the sign, the want to pet the adorable deer still strumming in my veins. Would a little nip hurt that hard? I bet I wouldn't even feel it through my glove.

Gabe grabs my arm, pulling me along. "You need your hands to catch the ball," he grumbles.

I can't help but smile, knowing he was clueing into what I was thinking.

"Want to take a picture with Santa?" I ask, eyeing a lineup.

Gabe rolls his eyes. "Aren't we a little old for that?"

I scoff. "Absolutely not. I *always* take a picture with Santa. However, I don't sit on his lap anymore. I'm kind of afraid I'll break him."

Gabe laughs at my words. It makes me happy to see him so at ease right now, especially after his confession about his parents. I'm happy that didn't kill the fun we're having tonight.

"How 'bout we take it together?" I suggest.

Gabe eyes me up for a minute but finally lifts a shoulder. "I'm already doing things outside my comfort zone tonight, so why not?"

A giddy rush thrums inside me, and without thinking, I grab his hand to pull him over to the line, hating that we have the barrier of our gloves between us. He laughs while I drag him along, not fighting my touch, which I take as a win. I'm kind of bummed when I have to pay the lady because I have to drop his hand. I already miss his hand in mine.

"Do you have any Christmas traditions with your nana?" I ask as we wait in line. We're lucky there are only a handful of people in front of us, considering it's already nine, and we still have an hour's drive ahead of us.

"On Christmas Eve, we watch Christmas movies, eat a crap ton of junk food, and wear matching pajamas," he supplies, his face lighting up as he talks.

"We do that too," I reply, loving that we are finding things in common, even if it's only Christmas traditions.

"Santa's ready to meet you," a lady dressed as an elf tells us with a giant smile, waving us through for our picture.

"Ho ho ho! Merry Christmas," Santa greets.

I wave at him. "Good to see you again, man. Thanks for

the football tickets last year." I wink at him, making him chuckle.

"I'm glad you liked them. What can I get you boys this year?"

I step closer to him and lean down to whisper in his ear. "Is making the cutie behind me my boyfriend too big of an ask?"

He laughs again and taps his nose. "I'll see what I can do. What about you, young man, what would you like for Christmas this year?" he asks Gabe.

Gabe shrugs, his cheeks brightening that gorgeous shade of pink, clearly not wanting to be the center of attention. "I've got all I need, but I wouldn't turn down a new book," he finally tells Santa.

"Ho ho ho!" Santa replies, grabbing his probably fake belly as he does. "A book is a marvelous present. I'll make sure that's under your tree this year."

"Picture time," the elf tells us, and I move to stand beside the jolly old man.

When Gabe goes to stand on Santa's other side, I stop him. "I might crush him, but you won't. You totally have to sit on his lap."

Gabe balks at me and shakes his head.

"Come on, young man, I won't bite," Santa encourages him. "And I promise I've had bigger boys than you sit on my lap."

Gabe purses his lips while he thinks about it, but he huffs out a breath and moves to sit on Santa's lap.

"That's the spirit," I cheer, then lean against Santa's giant chair as the lady takes our picture.

"Say cheese," she calls out.

As soon as the picture is taken, another elf guides us out, reminding us that our picture will be emailed to me within twenty-four hours.

We don't dawdle as much on our way back, clearly on a

mission to get to the car. We both have to wake up early in the morning for classes, but at the same time, I don't want the night to end. I'm having a blast with the cute nerd.

"I've got to use the bathroom. I'll meet you at the car," I tell Gabe once we are at the front. I hand him my keys, pretending I'm heading to the porta-potties.

Once he's out of sight, I return to the market tables to purchase the items I saw Gabe looking at longingly earlier.

Friends buy other friends gifts, right?

I shrug. There is no point in overthinking it. I want to buy these for him, so that's what I'm going to do, but maybe I'll hold onto them for a while so I don't scare him off tonight.

"What's in the bags?" Gabe asks when I slide into the driver's seat. "Do porta-potties have gift shops now?" he teases, and I find I really like this side of him.

I chuckle. "Nah. I remembered that my mom had been asking for some soap for a while. I figured the handmade ones at that one table would make a good Christmas gift," I tell him. Which isn't *entirely* a lie. It's just not the whole truth.

"That's sweet of you. Do you have any siblings?" he inquires.

"I've got a brother and two sisters," I reply. "I'm the oldest. What about you?"

"I'm an only child," he supplies, and I'm thankful there wasn't another person who was supposed to love him to turn their back on him.

"So you don't like sports, so what do you like?" I inquire, putting the car into drive.

"I love to read. My guilty pleasure is smutty gay romance books," he admits, and his cheeks brighten once again.

"Send me the name of your favorite book, and I'll give it a try."

"You like to read?" he asks, and I lift a shoulder.

"It's not something I normally do outside of textbooks, but I'm not opposed to widening my experiences. I'll try anything once," I say, shooting him a wink. "So besides reading, what else could I find you up to on a random night?"

"Sadly, my life is kind of boring. I work a lot, but if I'm not slinging drinks, I like to play board and video games with my roommates."

"I love video games. What's your favorite?" I ask, loving this conversation.

"It depends. I dabble in a lot, but last year, I kind of became obsessed with *Mario Kart* after a tutoring student of mine needed help connecting with his course load. Kind of like you," he states. "But I already knew a lot about *Mario Kart*. I didn't have to spend as much time researching as I did on you."

So he *did* put in extra work for me.

"We'll have to play *Mario Kart* sometime," I suggest.

"I think I'd like that," he whispers, bringing a smile to my lips.

"What's your favorite color?" I ask next.

He chuckles, and when I cast a quick glance at him, I almost regret it because his easy smile and bright brown eyes have my heart racing, making it extremely hard to focus on driving.

"Green, what about you?" he replies after I turn my eyes back to the road.

"Also green," I tell him and shoot him another wink. My eyes want to linger on his face, but I won't earn a second date if I get us into a car accident. Not that this is technically a date.

"What's your favorite animal?" he inquires. It almost makes me giddy that he's participating in asking questions, too, not only answering them.

"A koala, obviously," I reply, and I catch Gabe shaking his head out of the corner of my eye.

"Of course, what a silly question of me to ask," he teases.

"How about you? Or are you a secret koala lover as well?"

He chuckles, shaking his head again. "You do know koalas are riddled with chlamydia, right?" he checks.

I shrug. "They're still cute as fuck, but we're getting side-tracked here, what is your favorite animal?"

"If we're going based on cuteness, a fennec fox. If we're going based on lovability, you could still say a fennec fox, but a red panda is a close second," he responds.

Even though I'm just starting to get to know him, it makes so much sense that he didn't choose a basic animal like a cat or a dog. He didn't even choose a basic fox. He chose a very specific type—one I've never actually heard of, but still, it's just so him.

We spend the rest of the drive lobbing questions back and forth, and by the time I arrive at his house, I feel a real connection between us. I know we said this wasn't a date, but it feels like one to me. Does Gabe feel the same way?

"I had a blast tonight," he tells me after I put the car into park and turn toward him.

"Me too," I reply, and an awkward tension fills the small space.

What do we do now? If this *was* a date, I'd kiss him, but I don't want to cross the boundaries he's set. I want him to know I respect him.

Gabe looks out his window at the front of the plain house, not moving to get out of my car. It's not like I'm going to force him out. I'd sit here in awkward silence all night if that's what he wants. My attention stays fixed on him, waiting to find out what he's going to do next. His shoulders rise and fall as he takes a deep breath, then slowly turns back to me.

He stares at me intently for a few heartbeats, then with a speed I haven't seen from him, he launches himself at me, his lips landing on mine.

I thought for sure if this ever happened, it would be tenta-tive at first, but Gabe is giving me his all. Initially, I'm startled, but I quickly get ahold of myself and grab the back of his head to deepen the kiss.

A small whimper escapes his lips when I lick at the seam. He doesn't wait to give me entrance to his mouth, and I inwardly cheer when my tongue touches his. He tastes sweet, like the hot chocolate we sipped on at the light display.

Our tongues dance together as we make out, and my cock grows harder by the minute. Especially when he gets the courage to let his hands roam over my body—what he can reach in this awkward position in my car, anyway? Fuck, I want to feel his skin on mine. We ditched the gloves when we got into the car, but the barrier of my clothes still stops me from getting the full experience.

I lose track of time as we share this special moment. When he pulls back, I instantly miss his touch. We are both panting for air, and my dick throbs in my pants when I take in Gabe's kiss-swollen lips.

"This still wasn't a date," he whispers with a tiny smirk, but my brain must have short-circuited from the kiss because his words don't make sense.

"Wh-what?" I stammer, making Gabe chuckle.

He doesn't answer my question but gives me a quick peck on the lips, then opens the car door. "I'll see you Wednesday," he tells me before rushing into his house.

Well, shit. I can't believe that actually happened.

I know that no matter what Gabe says, that most definitely was a date, and I plan on earning another one soon.

CHAPTER ELEVEN

WHAT THE HELL *came over me in Chase's car?*

I close the door behind me as quietly as possible, praying that my roommates are already in bed, but of course, I don't have that kind of luck.

"Look what the cat dragged in," Victor teases, and I'm sure he has a shit-eating grin on his face, but I don't turn around. The moment I do, he'll see my kiss swollen lips, and the ribbing will *really* start.

I've never launched myself at someone like that. I've never run my hands up and down someone's sides as we steamed up the car windows. I'm not a virgin, but maybe I was a prude because the only time I ever let someone get even remotely physical with me was behind closed doors in a bedroom. Public displays of affection made my skin crawl, yet every time Chase's hand brushed against mine, I wondered what it would be like to stop the game and take hold of his. Unfortunately, I wasn't brave enough to do that. But while we were sitting in his car, I knew I couldn't end the night with a wave or a handshake. Even a hug wouldn't have satisfied me. So, I pushed my fears to the side and took a chance—one that thankfully paid off.

Chase's lips were just as swollen as I'm sure mine were when we parted, and it took everything in me to open the car door and say goodnight, which is not like me at all.

"Did you finally say yes to a date with the sexy quarterback?" Sasha asks.

I don't reply while I hang up my coat, knowing that when my friends see my face, it will be all the answer they need.

When I finally turn, Sasha gasps, but an evil smirk slowly spreads across his face. "I'm so glad you finally came to your senses. Please tell me that your lips aren't the only thing he sucked tonight."

I roll my eyes at my friend's antics. "Not everyone puts out on the first date," I reply with a shrug.

Victor nods in solidarity. "Not everyone is a slut like you," he tells Sasha, who, of course, takes his words as a compliment.

"I know, not everyone can be as amazing as me," he replies with a big-ass grin before turning his full attention back to me. "Where did he take you? Was he a gentleman? Did he pin you against his car and suck your face?"

I shake my head, but I can't force away the smile spreading across my face. "He took me to this Christmas Village thing. There was this amazing light tunnel, and we even got our picture taken with Santa," I inform them.

"*You* got your picture taken with Santa?" Victor asks, sounding shocked. I guess his reaction is warranted.

I'm not normally the type of person to do things like that. I think it's because I hate to be the center of attention. I usually want to blend into the background and let people forget I exist. But Chase is the exact opposite. He loves all eyes on him. His energy was contagious. The way his face lit up with so much joy and excitement at the idea of the silly photo had me throwing caution to the wind and doing whatever he wanted me to do. There was no way I could have told him no, even if I wanted to, which I don't think I really did. I actually enjoyed the experience, even if sitting on a random stranger's lap was a bit uncomfortable. What other things would I do with Chase by my side?

"What?" I ask, feigning ignorance. "Can't a couple of guys take a photo with Santa?"

"Normal people, yes. *You?* Not so much," Sasha states, then leans toward Victor and stage whispers, "Maybe he's been abducted by an alien."

"If you two are done hounding me on my evening, I'm going to go to bed," I tell them, stepping around them to head to the stairs.

"We're not done, but we'll let you sleep and pick up this lovely conversation in the morning," Victor says. "I know Max is going to want in on this."

I shake my head but don't bother responding. I'd like to say I hope my friends will forget about this conversation by morning, but I know, without a shadow of a doubt, they won't. But I don't blame them because if this was happening to any of them, I'd be all over that shit and wanting every last detail.

Once I'm in my room, I drop my bag by the door and strip out of my clothes before throwing myself onto my bed. When I close my eyes, the memory of the kiss tonight replays in my mind. My cock grows in my underwear, and I shove my hand inside, giving myself a long, slow stroke. My head falls back, and my lips part as a needy mewl escapes.

I continue to stroke myself and daydream about what might have happened had I been brave enough to invite Chase in.

"You're so fucking hot," Chase tells me, pushing me onto the bed, joining me instantly.

We're both naked. I'm not sure how, but this is a daydream, so who cares about semantics?

"I want to taste you," Chase tells me, lowering himself down my body and leaving a trail of kisses, licks, and nibbles as he goes.

A gasp is pulled from my lips when he finally gets to my needy cock.

Chase's tongue is warm and wet as he licks me from root to tip. My toes curl, and my fingers grasp at the sheets.

"Don't be afraid to touch me, baby," he tells me with intense eyes and a sexy smirk before he engulfs me in his hot mouth.

My head falls back, and I lift my hand to thread my fingers through his hair as I cry out with pleasure. My breathing is shallow, and my heart is beating so fast I'm almost afraid I am going to pass out.

Like everything Chase does, he's confident and sure as he sucks me into his mouth and swallows me down. The constriction of his throat has me bucking into him, needing more and less at the same time.

"Fuck," I shout when he begins to bob up and down.

He's sloppy about the blow job but in the most delicious way possible. Spit mixed with precum drools out of the corners of his mouth, trailing down my dick toward my balls.

I stroke my cock faster, lost in the daydream, wishing it was reality.

"You taste so fucking good," Chase tells me, coming up for air. "Think you can fill my mouth with your delicious load?"

I nod, my mind going blank. I'm unable to come up with words, which might be a first for me.

With that, Chase dives back in, blowing me with precise move-ments. There's no doubt about it. He knows what he is doing, and it won't take long before I come.

A layer of sweat covers my body, and a tingle forms at the base of my spine as my orgasm draws near. Chase slides his hand between his legs, jerking himself off at the same pace that he's bobbing up and down on me. I can't take my eyes off him. It's so fucking hot.

When his eyes meet mine again, it's like he's smirking at me and gives a slight nod as if pleading for me to come, and do I ever.

"Jesus. Fucking. Christ," I yell so loud my lungs burn and explode down Chase's throat. He swallows every last drop, continuing to suck me until I'm almost pleading for him to stop.

"Let me take care of you," I request once he lets me go.

He shakes his head with a cocky grin. "Don't worry about it. The second I tasted you, I blew my load."

I jolt upright as my real-life orgasm takes over, and I paint my stomach in a layer of cum. My breathing is rapid and shallow as I ride out the high. I've never come this hard in my entire life. If just a daydream could give me such an intense orgasm, what would the real-life thing be like?

It could only be better.

My head falls against the bed again, and I let my breathing even out before eventually climbing out of bed to clean up myself. Using a towel on my floor, I wipe myself down, wrap it around my waist, and rush to the bathroom for a quick shower. It's a miracle I don't run into any of my roommates along the way.

I discard the used towel into the hamper once I'm in the confines of the bathroom and grab a clean towel out of the closet.

My heart is still beating fast when I step into the shower, and my head is foggy. How the hell did I go from not wanting to date Chase to having a fantasy-driven orgasm about him?

I can no longer deny that I'm into Chase. And now I also know that we have things in common.

I just pray that by taking this plunge, it doesn't come back to bite me in the ass.

CHAPTER TWELVE

SATURDAYS USED to be my favorite day, but Wednesdays are quickly taking that place, along with Sundays. Any day I'm able to see Gabe is the best day.

There's an extra pep in my step as I head toward the library, but it isn't just because I'm about to see the guy I am kind of crazy about. It's also because we got our newest assignment handed back today, and I got a passing grade. My first one of the semester. My professor even told me if I kept up the hard work, not only would I stay above the minimum, but my final grade should be well above passing. I was beyond excited. I might have earned myself a headshake from my professor when I jumped up and fist-bumped the air shouting, 'yes' over and over again, but he also had a smile on his lips, so I know he wasn't too irritated with me.

I gave my coach the good news at practice this afternoon. He told me how proud of me he was, which also stroked my ego, making for a really fantastic day overall. And it's only going to get better because I'm on my way to see Gabe.

When I enter the library, I head to the second floor and toward the back, where my sexy tutor is waiting. "Hey, handsome, I've missed you this week," I tell him with a wink, dropping my bag to the floor and pulling out my chair.

"Why would you do something silly like that?" he asks

with a raised brow, the corners of his lips twitching while he fights a smile.

"I'm not sure. Maybe it's because you gave me a kiss that was fucking hard to forget the other night," I inform him.

His cheeks pinken, and the smile finally breaks free. "Stop flirting. It's time to study," he scolds, but there's no heat behind his words.

"Can I flirt once we're done studying?" I ask.

He sighs, but his grin grows. "I suppose."

I internally give myself a high five, then move to grab my textbook and the graded assignment. "Check this out," I cheer, handing over the piece of paper.

The way his face lights up fills me with even more pride. "This is amazing, Chase. We've only been working together for about two weeks, and you're already turning things around. I told you you weren't dumb."

My cheeks hurt from how widely I'm smiling, and the tips of my ears warm. I'm not one who gets embarrassed by compliments, but Gabe's praise is causing me to be a bit bashful.

"But one passing assignment isn't enough, so let's work on your next one," he instructs, and I nod, pulling out my laptop.

I mostly work on my assignment by myself, but Gabe is there whenever I have a question. Being in his presence gives me the confidence I have never felt before in this course.

"Can I flirt now?" I ask after we've finished our hour of studying.

Gabe chuckles and lifts a shoulder. "Would you stop if I said no?" he asks.

I put my finger on my chin and stare at the ceiling as if deeply thinking about his question before shaking my head. "I don't think so."

He laughs again, and I can't help but join in this time.

"You're a really great kisser," I tell him, loving the way he blushes.

"You're not so bad yourself," he murmurs.

"What are you up to tomorrow night?" I check.

"Working," he grumbles, his smile fading a little.

"Do you not like your job?" I inquire.

Gabe shakes his head. "It's not that. The job itself is fine. I'm just tired. It's not cheap putting yourself through college, even with my scholarship."

My heart aches a little for him. I can't even begin to wonder what it's like because I've never had that struggle. My scholarship covers my living expenses. Even if it didn't, my parents would help cover them while I'm here. I hate that Gabe doesn't have that kind of support, but a lot of students don't.

"Want to grab a bite to eat?" I ask, not wanting to say goodbye yet.

"I suppose I could eat," he replies, putting his supplies away.

"Can we call this a date, or are we still just friends?" I inquire as we walk out of the library. "Because I'm not sure about you, but I've never kissed a friend the way we kissed the other night."

His cheeks pinken again, and he shakes his head. "I don't kiss most people the way I kissed you," he whispers. "Obviously, I was fighting whatever this is, but you make me feel like a different person. I like it." My chest puffs out a little at his admission, and I love that I'm able to make him feel like that.

"What's going on tomorrow?" he asks as we head to my car.

"My best friend, Rio, is playing in round one of the championships for soccer. I know you aren't a sports guy, but I figured you could meet my friends this way," I tell him.

"You want to introduce me to your friends already?" His eyes are wide, like the idea is absurd.

"Why wouldn't I?"

He shrugs. "I don't know. I guess I'm still a little shocked that a guy like you would want to date me. Maybe a part of me was thinking you were going to want to keep this on the down-low."

I stop walking and put my hands on Gabe's shoulders. "You're not a dirty little secret, and if anyone has ever made you feel like that, they deserve to rot in hell. I like you, Gabe. I'm not afraid to let anyone know that. Besides, my friends are already well aware of my feelings for you."

His pretty mouth parts, and he stares at me for a moment. "Do you really mean that?"

I nod. "Absolutely. I've never been one to lie."

Taking a chance, I lean in and press my lips to his, even though we are standing in the library's parking lot. Anyone could see us, but that's kind of the point. I want him to know I'm not ashamed of him.

The kiss is simple since I don't want to get in trouble for public indecency because if it turns into anything like the other night, I won't be able to keep my hands to myself. The thought has me biting back a moan. And my breath catches when Gabe melts into me, his arms wrapping around me to pull me closer. He licks at my lips, and it almost does me in. I have to take him somewhere else soon, or we're both going to be in a lot of trouble. It takes almost all of my strength to break the kiss, and I don't miss the way Gabe pouts when I do so.

"Would you like to come back to my apartment for a little bit?" I whisper against his lips, praying I'm not being too forward.

"I'd like that," he replies quietly, which brings a giant smile to my lips.

I grab his hand and pull him to my car, walking a little faster than earlier.

Gabe chuckles and squeezes my hand. "Slow down, you big oaf. Not everyone has long legs like you," he chastises playfully.

"I could carry you," I suggest, earning me a cute glare.

"Try it, and I'll show you that even short people can cause bodily damage. If you like your balls attached to your body, I suggest you keep my feet on the ground. While we're in public, anyway." The end of his sentence comes out barely audible, but I hear it, and it has my cock aching.

I slow my steps so Gabe doesn't have to run to keep up with me.

"Do you have roommates?" Gabe asks once we are in front of my car.

"Two of them. Rio, the soccer player, his real name is Arthur Leon, by the way, but it's a long story about how he got his nickname, and Brett Henderson, who plays football with me, but everyone calls him Hendo."

"What is it with you jocks and the weird nicknames?" he inquires.

I lift a shoulder. "It's just something the majority of us do. It's kind of like a rite of passage once you earn your nickname. Most guys are just abbreviations of their last names, but some have fun ones because they did something memorable. Like Rio and my buddy, Teddy."

"How is Teddy a nickname based on something memorable?" Gabe questions.

I smirk at him. "His real name is Brendon Morgan. He got the nickname because he lost his teddy bear one day when we were playing an away game. He freaked out and had the entire team searching for it. He swore he couldn't play without being able to sleep with the damn thing the night before. I'm not sure if you know this or not, but athletes can be very superstitious," I inform him before continuing the story. "We eventually found it at the front desk of the hotel lobby. It must have fallen out of his bag. The receptionist assumed it belonged to a child. She almost didn't want to turn it over to the bunch of jocks, but Brendon eventually convinced her it was his, and the rest is kind of history. Now, the only name he really goes by is Teddy. I haven't heard his real name in years."

"That's actually kind of awesome… the creative ones, anyway. The last-name ones are still a bit stupid," he mumbles.

I laugh. "You're not wrong, but it would be hard to come up with creative ones for everybody. I mean, some people are kind of boring."

Gabe chuckles. "How did you end up with a last name nickname? And don't tell me it's because you're boring. I know that's not true."

I smile at him and nod. "True, I'm definitely not boring, but I've had my nickname since middle school when I wasn't as outgoing. It was easy to just stick with it. But nicknames are open to change, so who knows, maybe I'll do something batshit crazy one day and earn a new one."

"I've never had a nickname," he whispers. "And I usually insist people call me by my full name, but when you called me Gabe earlier this evening, it didn't make my skin crawl like it normally does. I actually liked it."

"If you want me to call you Gabriel, I will," I assure him.

He shakes his head. "No, I like it when you do it. It feels special."

I grin at him. "I like that I'm the only one you let call you it."

The drive to my apartment is quick, and when we get out of my car, I grab Gabe's hand again, wanting to touch him in any way I can.

"This is a nice place," Gabe notes as we make our way to the third floor.

"Thanks, a lot of GSU athletes live in this building since it's super close to campus."

Gabe nods. "Yeah, I lucked out being able to live at Victor's house. I don't have a car, so being within walking distance is necessary."

"It must still suck when there's a blizzard, though," I reply, and he shrugs.

"It's not ideal, but I'd rather spend my money on food and living expenses than a car."

Sometimes I forget how privileged I am. My parents bought me my car as a graduation present, and I never thought twice about it. Maybe that makes me an asshole, but it wasn't out of malice. Now that I'm dating Gabe, I do feel like a dick for not being more grateful. At least that's something I can change.

Reaching my apartment, I let us in, and Gabe takes in where I live. As he looks around, I take a second to see this place through new eyes. The main living area is simple with cream walls, two oversized leather couches, a big-ass television with a killer sound system, and all the gaming consoles a guy could ask for. The kitchen is off the living area, with a breakfast bar separating the two spaces.

"Welcome to my humble abode," I say.

"Who are you talking to?" Hendo asks, coming out of his room. His eyes go wide when they land on Gabe. "You must be the tutor. I'm the better-looking roommate, Brett, but you can call me Hendo."

Gabe blushes, and I hate that he's doing it for him. My back molars grind together, and I huff out a breath.

Hendo laughs, but Gabe looks confused. "Are you okay?" he whispers.

"He's fine, just jealous," Hendo supplies and has the audacity to wink at Gabe.

I growl at him, which only makes him laugh harder.

Gabe squeezes my hand and leans into me, reassuring me with his body that he's there with me, not Hendo.

"Is Rio already asleep?" I check, and Hendo nods.

"He needs as much rest as possible for the first big game tomorrow," he replies.

"Makes sense. Well, now that you seem to be done flirting with my date…" I growl out, "… let me properly introduce the two of you. Brett, this is Gabriel. Gabe, this is my idiot friend and roommate, Brett."

Gabe chuckles and reaches out his hand to Hendo. "It's nice to meet you. You can flirt all you want, but I'm not usually one to go for jocks…" He pauses and points his thumb toward me. "This one is the exception."

I shoot Hendo a cocky grin, then wrap my arm around Gabe's shoulder. "Take that," I goad my friend, sticking my tongue out at him. "If you need us, we'll be in my room. *Don't need us.*"

Hendo laughs at me as I guide Gabe down the hall.

"I got the best bedroom," I say, opening the door. "It's the only one with an en suite, so I don't have to share with my knuckle-head friends."

"How did you get so lucky to snag this room?" he asks, and I can't help but snicker at the memory that pops up.

"We had a competition," I start. "Whoever could eat the most hot wings in an hour got the room."

Gabe laughs, shaking his head. "How many did you manage to eat?"

"I only needed to eat fifty. The other two tapped out at that point. I'm pretty sure I could have managed a hundred easily, though."

I won't bring up how rotten my guts would be after eating that many hot wings. I don't need to kill the mood before we even get started.

"I was wondering when I was going to see your personality shine in your apartment," Gabe muses out loud, taking in my space.

"We all agreed to keep the main living areas neutral zones, but our bedrooms were a free-for-all," I explain.

He nods, staring at my mini trophy shelf. I didn't bring all my trophies with me when I moved in because it would be kind of pointless since I won't live here forever, but I wanted to have the special ones.

"Is this a bowling trophy?" Gabe asks with a smirk.

"Damn right. I got that when I was six," I tell him, picking it up and taking it with me while I move to sit on the bed.

Gabe joins me, leaning into me. *Damn, I really like having him here.*

"My dad decided he wanted to try bowling, but my mom thought it was boring, and my other siblings weren't old enough, so I became his partner. We went three nights a week, and I loved it. But it wasn't the sport that I loved the most. I loved spending time with my dad. It didn't hurt that I was naturally talented at it, either. My dad, however, was not. But he also enjoyed spending time with me. After one year of bowling three nights a week, my dad entered me into a kid's championship, and I won this." I shake the trophy in my hand. "There were only ten of us, so the competition wasn't that steep, but it was the first trophy I ever won, and I did it with my dad by my side. This one is always going to mean the most to me."

"That's really sweet," Gabe remarks, and I set the trophy down.

"What can I say? I'm like an onion. I've got many layers. Sweet is just one of them."

Gabe laughs. "Is corny one as well?"

I shrug, pursing my lips. "Maybe."

We sit there silently for a moment or two, and I contemplate what I should do. I don't want to just jump him. That doesn't feel right, and I'm also afraid it will make him run.

"Can I kiss you again?" I ask, unable to stand the silence anymore.

Gabe beams at me. "I'd love that."

Before I kiss him, I gently remove his glasses, setting them on my nightstand. Then I press my lips to his, my hand coming up to caress his face. He sighs and leans into me more, and with my other hand, I grab his hip, encouraging him to straddle me.

"Do you have any idea what you do to me?" he whispers against my lips. "I'm normally so calculated, yet you break me out of my shell, and it doesn't even terrify me."

I smile. "I'm different around you too. I've never had to chase after anyone, and I never would have wanted to before I met you. The moment I met you, I knew you were someone I wanted to get to know better, and now that you're here in my arms, I don't think I'll ever want to let you go."

"Can you promise me something?" he asks, and I nod.

"Anything."

"Don't break my heart," he pleads.

"I would never," I assure him before smashing my lips back to his.

He moans into my mouth, and I take the opening to slide in my tongue. He grinds his hips into me, his hard cock pressing against my stomach. There are far too many layers between us, and I'm desperate to have my hands on his skin.

"Can we get rid of some of these barriers?" I ask, grabbing the hem of his shirt.

"Absolutely," he agrees eagerly and helps me remove his shirt.

Once his torso is bare, I strip out of my shirt and wrap my arms around him once again, my hands gliding up and down his lean back.

"Wow, how many abs do you have?" Gabe asks, staring at my stomach.

"A solid eight-pack, baby," I brag with a smirk.

"I must look like a twig to you," he mumbles, moving to cover his body with his arms, but I stop him.

"Don't hide from me," I beg. "I don't care if you have a ripped body. I think you're sexy just the way you are."

He nibbles on his lower lip but slowly nods. "If you say so," he whispers.

I lick at his lower lip, finally bringing a smile to his gorgeous face. "I do say so. I told you I don't lie."

In a swift motion Gabe doesn't expect, I flip us around so that he is lying on the bed, and I'm hovering over him. Then I lean down to devour his mouth once more. I can't get enough of this guy. He's so fucking delicious, and right now, he's mine.

I grind my hips into his so he can feel my desire for him, even with the current barriers.

"Too... many... clothes..." Gabe pants out, whimpering beneath me. "I want to feel all of you."

We're on the exact same page, and my cock throbs in agreement.

I climb off him and undo my jeans as he rids himself of the rest of his clothes at the same time. Once I'm finally free of the confines of my clothes and am standing in front of him, naked as the day I was born, I don't move. I just stare at the man lying in front of me. He's so fucking gorgeous like this. His skin flushed with desire, and his hard dick lays against his stomach. He's a lot larger than I thought he was going to be, and my mouth waters with a desire to devour him *now*.

"You're making me anxious," Gabe murmurs while I continue to take him in.

I chuckle and finally move toward him again, crawling on the bed. "Sorry, I didn't mean to make you anxious," I tell him, running my hand up his side, causing goose bumps to erupt on his skin. "I just wanted to spend a minute taking in how fucking hot you are."

Being naked with Gabe is like a dirty dream come true,

and the way he reacts to my touch has my cock throbbing between my legs. I'm going to have to be careful that I don't come prematurely.

His smile is bashful, and his cheeks are the pinkest I've ever seen them.

Slowly, I lean in to kiss him while my hands continue to roam over his sides. As much as I love kissing his mouth, I'm desperate to know every inch of his body, so I move away from his lips, trailing kisses along his jaw to his earlobe that I suck into my mouth. Gabe's back bows off the bed when I graze my teeth across it, and I smile at how responsive he is.

After another nibble of his ear, I move down to his neck, kissing, licking, sucking, exploring. I take my time making my way down his body until my nose is buried in his groin, breathing in his unique scent. It's citrusy with a hint of musk. I stick my tongue out to lick him, close to where he wants my mouth but still far away. The saltiness of his sweat clings to my tongue. How does he always taste so fucking good? And if just his skin can have my cock leaking, what the hell is his cum going to do to me?

I'm desperate to find out.

With a turn of my head, I'm lined up with his cock, and I take a long slow lick of him, from root to tip. When I get to the top, I stick my tongue into his slit and groan at how fucking delicious he is.

"Jesus," Gabe groans out, and I wink at him.

"I'm going to give you the best blow job you've ever had," I promise him. "But make sure you stay quiet. Your sounds are only for me. I don't need my roommates getting off on them."

Gabe's lips part, and his eyelids are heavy with lust, but he nods.

With a smirk, I dive down and swallow him as far as I can take him. His breath hitches when he hits the back of my throat, which only encourages me to try and take more of him in. Relaxing my jaw a little more, I swallow him down, gagging a little, but I know how fucking good that feels on a cock so I'm positive the sexy nerd in my bed won't be complaining.

I'm sloppy as I blow him, covering him in my saliva. The room is quiet except for the sound of my slurping, gagging, and Gabe's heavy breathing.

"Damn, you're good at that," he whispers in an awe-filled tone. "Even better than my dreams."

"You've been dreaming about me, baby?" I ask, taking a small break to catch my breath.

He blushes again, but most of his body is now a beautiful shade of pink from his elevated heart rate.

"I have been, and I was wondering if we could try something," he mentions quietly.

I dip my chin, eager to hear what he has in mind. "I'm all ears, baby. What do you want to try?"

"You're fucking amazing at sucking cock, but I'm desperate to taste you too. I want to feel your cock filling my mouth. I want to know what your load tastes like. Could we try sixty-nining?" he inquires.

His words have my cock dribbling precum against the bedding. Jesus, I wasn't expecting him to say that, but I'm all for it. "That sounds like heaven. Do you want me on top or you on top?"

It will probably be best if Gabe's on top because I'm not sure I'll be able to control myself from destroying his throat if it's the other way around, but I'll do whatever this gorgeous man wants. I'll just have to pray to some kind of deity for self-control the size of a Mac truck.

"Would you mind if I go on top?" he asks.

I smile, moving beside him, thankful I bought the king-size bed. "Whatever you want," I assure him.

He nibbles his lower lip, then moves to climb on top of me, his gorgeous cock hanging proudly in front of my face. I stick my tongue out to lick the tip, and he lets out a little gasp. But I'm the one who's groaning like a wild animal as his warm, wet mouth engulfs me, and he takes me all the way down his throat. *Holy fucking shitballs.* Gabe doesn't have a gag reflex.

My eyes roll into the back of my head as he swallows, and the already tight channel constricts around my aching dick. "Shiiittt," I grit out through my teeth.

Gabe's hips wiggle with what I think is pride, but it also reminds me that I have a job to do. I open my lips and suck the head of Gabe's crown into my mouth, suckling him briefly, which results in him groaning around me, the vibrations shooting directly to my balls. I've never been a two-pump chump, but this man and his very talented mouth are about to make me come quicker than I ever have in my life. Well, maybe not faster than when I was a teenager playing with myself for the first time, but still *really* damn fast.

Wanting Gabe to come with me, I hollow my cheeks and start to suck him like a hoover. I grip his hips and fight against my gag reflex to take him all the way. I swallow and begin to gag, so I pull back even though I wish I could keep him deep in my throat.

The noises are a little louder, more slurping and gagging, but now they're joined by muffled moans of pleasure.

My balls tingle, cueing me that I'm about to lose it, so I tap Gabe's side, alerting him that if he doesn't want a mouthful of jizz, now would be the time to move, but he doesn't. In fact, he does the opposite, pushing farther down, swallowing again and *again*, those last constrictions finally sending me over the edge. I come so hard it's hard to breathe. However, that also might be the fact that I have a cock in my mouth too.

While Gabe swallows every last drop, he lets go and starts to fuck my face, which I love. It has my spent cock wanting to come back to life again already. Twenty-year-olds are known for their stamina, but that's extra fucking quick, even for a young guy like me.

Laying back, I let Gabe use me, trying to keep with my sucks and licks as best as I can.

"I-I'm going to come," Gabe gasps out in warning.

I grip his hips firmly, wordlessly telling him to do it—to fill my mouth with his load and let me have every last drop I'm so fucking desperate for. When I suck him as hard as I can, he finally lets go, and his warm cum coats my tongue. He buries his face into the mattress between my legs, using it to muffle his shouts of pleasure.

This intense pridefulness fills my chest. I fucking did that to him. Me. I got him to lose control. It's obvious Gabe doesn't let that happen often, but I was able to push him over the ledge tonight, and I goddamn loved it.

Gabe's hips jerk, making it hard to swallow without gagging again, but the taste of him and knowing I have this kind of control over him makes it worth it. With one final jolt, his legs trembling, he pulls out, slumping next to me.

"Can I hold you for a minute?" I ask quietly.

Gabe turns around and leans his head on my chest. "You're a cuddler, aren't you?" he murmurs.

I nod before kissing his forehead. "Is that a bad thing?" I check, wrapping my arm around his body.

He doesn't respond right away. His fingers dance through my treasure trail as he lies silently by my side. *What is going through his head?* Thankfully, he doesn't leave me wondering for long.

"I've never been a touchy-feely kind of guy. Cuddling always felt awkward," he whispers, his hot breath cascading across my chest. "But it feels nice with you."

A giant grin spreads across my lips, and I hold him a little tighter because this moment isn't going to last forever. Part of me wants to ask him to spend the night, but I'm also worried that would be too much too fast for him, and if he said no, the rejection would surely bruise me.

"I should probably get going," he murmurs after God only knows how long passes in comfortable silence.

"You don't have to, you know," I offer.

Gabe pushes his upper body up, and there is a small smile on his lips as he leans in for a kiss. "I've never wanted to sleep in the same bed as someone before," he tells me, his lips moving against mine. "But if I didn't have a commitment tomorrow morning, I would stay."

My face hurts from how big I'm smiling, and Gabe chuckles while hitting my chest gently. "Wipe that silly grin off your face," he complains teasingly, trying to fight his own goofy smile.

"Can't, you just admitted I'm special. Coming from the guy who was bound and determined that we had nothing in common."

He rolls his eyes but doesn't argue.

"Can I see you before Sunday?" I inquire while he moves to put his clothes back on.

Damn, I already miss the feeling of him in my arms. That's a new one for me. Yes, I'm a cuddler, but usually, when it's over, it is what it is. I don't miss the person's body pressed against mine.

"I'm pretty busy with work, school, my other tutoring students, and my own studies, but we can try to make something work," he tells me.

I have to fight the urge to fist-bump the air. I still can't believe I'm winning him over so fast. But I'm not one to look a fed horse in the mouth or whatever the hell that damn saying is.

I throw on a pair of sweats and my GSU hoodie, then grab my car keys off the dresser, earning me a weird look from Gabe.

"What?" I look around, rubbing at my face.

Why is he staring at me like that?

"Why did you grab your car keys?" he asks, leaving my room.

"Because I'm going to drive you home," I answer slowly, a little confused by his question.

His brows are pulled together, and he looks just as confused as I feel. "Why?"

"Because I drove us here, and you live on the other side of the campus. Were you expecting me to make you walk?" I inquire.

Gabe tips his head from side to side. "Honestly, I'm not sure."

I step toward him, and he lifts his chin to stare into my eyes. "I don't know if you've dated assholes in the past or you think I'm going to be a jerk because I'm a jock, but I was raised right. So, I'm going to drive you home, and I don't want to hear any arguments."

His eyes are wide, and his lips part like he's shocked at my words, but eventually, he dips his chin.

"Let's get going then," I say, tilting my head toward the door.

I make a silent vow to myself as I drive Gabe home that I'm going to show him how he deserves to be treated. I don't like the insecurities that shadow behind his eyes. If I have to battle his demons for him, I'm willing to do so.

CHAPTER THIRTEEN

Gabriel

THERE IS a dopey smile on my face as I make my morning coffee that won't go away no matter how hard I try. Last night was fucking perfect. I've never had sex that good in my entire life. And the orgasm was even better than the multiples I had thinking about Chase late at night, which were ridiculously intense.

But what threw me for the biggest loop was how my skin didn't crawl when Chase held me. There was no urge to run away. I actually enjoyed being in his arms and didn't want to leave. What is it about Chase that makes me feel like this?

"How are you so happy at an ungodly time like this?" Sasha grumbles, his feet shuffling against the kitchen floor.

Normally, I would correct him that it isn't that early, but today he's right. It's four-thirty in the morning. Most normal people are still sleeping, but we're awake so we can be good citizens.

Once a month, my roommates and I volunteer at a youth center, serving breakfast to kids and teens before they go to school. Only a fraction of the kids we serve breakfast to live at the youth center. The rest are just poor kids who need a helping hand and want a hot breakfast.

When I graduate from law school, it's kids and families like them I want to help—the people the majority of the world wants to forget about. I considered that being a social worker and lawyer would let me help more people in the long run.

"Why is Gabriel smiling like that?" Victor asks as he and Max enter the kitchen at the same time.

"He's been possessed by an alien," Sasha mutters.

"You get abducted by aliens and possessed by ghosts," I correct him, then pour everyone a thermos of coffee.

"Tomayto, tomahto," Sasha replies.

"Does this smile have anything to do with the fact that you were very late coming home from your tutoring session last night?" Max checks with a shit-eating grin on his face.

I roll my eyes and sigh. "If you must know…" I pause, and they all lean in more like the tea-thirsty whores that they are. "I had sex with Chase last night."

All three of their brows shoot sky-high.

"Well, damn," Victor whispers.

"I'm fucking proud of you," Sasha declares and pats me on the shoulder, knowing I'm not the biggest for physical affection. Or wasn't—I don't mind it now. No, that's wrong. I still don't love it unless it comes from a certain quarterback who is quickly worming his way into my life in a manner I wasn't expecting.

"It was just sex," I grumble, but my stupid smile remains firmly on my face.

"Maybe, but you're radiating this joy I'm not sure I've ever seen from you before," Max notes.

"Are you calling me a grump?" I challenge.

He laughs and shakes his head. "No, but you're controlled. You like things a *very* particular way and don't stray from the path you've set out for yourself. Ever since you met Chase, you're changing, which is a good thing."

I don't argue with him because he's right. I am changing, and that scares the shit out of me. The reason I don't stray from my path is because it's terrifying. There are so many unknowns when I stray from the path, things I can't control. I don't like the unexpected, and this new relationship with Chase is filled with things I won't be able to predict. In any other situation, that would make me sick to my stomach, but that's not how I'm feeling right now. I'm exhilarated and excited for what's to come. Yes, there are still nerves, but they aren't as debilitating as they usually would be.

"Who's ready to serve breakfast to underprivileged kids?" I ask after a moment of silence and hand each of my friends a thermos.

"He's still the king of deflecting," Victor mumbles with a smirk.

Shrugging, I head to the front door to put on my coat, and the rest of the guys follow. Once we're ready, we head to Max's car and make our way to the youth center.

The drive isn't long, only a half hour at this time of the morning. It will be longer on the way back, but we will make sure to budget our time accordingly so we won't be late for classes. The entire way, I keep thinking back to last night. The way Chase looked at me with hungry eyes. The way he sucked my dick like he was a starved man. The way he held me like I was a cherished jewel.

I'm going to have to be careful with my heart when it comes to this man. But he promised me he isn't a liar, and I don't have any reason not to trust him. Maybe one of these nights, we can talk about what's happening between us. Am I just a passing fling to him, or is he willing to see where this goes? But where exactly *can* this go? I've done some research on his football stats, and there is a strong possibility he will be drafted into the NFL in the spring. If I let myself fall for him, there is a huge chance my heart will end up shattered, not because Chase is a bad guy but because we're on two different life paths.

I push the depressing thoughts aside when we arrive at the youth center. There's no point in dwelling on the what-ifs right now, especially when I don't know what we are.

A bunch of rowdy, smiling kids greet us when we walk through the front doors, and I wave at the familiar faces before heading to the front desk to sign in.

"Good morning, gentlemen. How are you this fine November morning?" Sheila, the facility coordinator, asks us.

"Cold," Sasha replies, making her laugh.

"Oh, sweetie, you know this is nothing," she reminds him. "Just wait until we're hit with a December blizzard. Then, you'll be wishing for balmy days like today."

"Tell that to my shriveled-up balls," he grumbles under his breath so quietly that I'm pretty sure she doesn't hear him, which was probably the point.

I shake my head at him but don't blame the guy for complaining. He's from California. Their winters are nothing like the ones we experience here. I always wondered why he chose GSU when California has some great law schools, but when I asked him, he told me he wanted a change in scenery. However, his answer didn't feel one hundred percent truthful, but I didn't want to pressure him into telling me more. If he wanted to share, he would.

Sheila guides us to the kitchen, setting each of us up at a station, not bothering to give us extra directions. We've been coming here for over two years and know what we're doing. The only time things change a little is when the kids are off from school. And Thanksgiving is still a week away, so we don't have to worry about that now.

Today, I'm on serving duty, smiling at each kid passing by me. Volunteering at the youth center is something that fills my soul. I know what it's like to be an outcast, and my family wasn't far off from needing a place like this when I was a kid. I could have used a listening ear or even just a smile from someone who wasn't being paid to be nice to me. If I can give that to even just *one* of these kids, I've done my job.

Breakfast flies by in a blur like it always does, and before I know it, we're back in Max's car on our way home. By the time we arrive at the house, I'll have just enough time to grab my backpack and run to class.

I'm a bit of a control freak when it comes to being on time, my skin crawling if I'm even a second late, but even all the anxiety in the world couldn't keep me away from those kids. They're worth the possibility of being late, which isn't going to happen today by the looks of things, which is an added bonus.

The second Max parks the car, I rush out to grab my backpack from where I left it by the front door and wave at my friends as I rush to class.

On my way to class, my phone buzzes in my pocket, and I pull it out, smiling at Chase's name on the screen.

> Chase: I know you're working tonight, but what are you up to tomorrow?

I contemplate how I should respond. Should I play it cool? But how exactly does one play it cool?

I give my head a shake. As usual, I'm overthinking things.

> Me: I'm working in the evening, but I have tomorrow morning off.

His response is instant, which definitely fits the guy I'm getting to know.

Chase: Awesome! Me too! Want to have a breakfast date?

My smile grows as I type out my response.

Me: Okay.

Chase: Yes! I'll pick you up at eight if that's all right.

Me: Sounds good. See you tomorrow.

Chase: *kissy face emoji*

I chuckle, then notice the time and pick up my pace. I can't let a boy be the reason I'm late for class.

Even if he does give me butterflies.

CHAPTER FOURTEEN

Chase

THE MORNING AIR has a bite to it, but nothing could wipe the smile off my face, not even a blizzard, which, thankfully, there isn't one.

Pulling up to Gabe's house, I freeze. Should I go to the door or not? Normally, it would be a no-brainer, but he gave me shit at his nana's house the one time. But that wasn't an official date. That's what he scolded me about. Today, however, is.

"Fuck it," I whisper to myself and get out of the car.

Excited energy courses through my veins as I take the steps to the front door and knock.

"You must be the quarterback," a tall, slender man with long, blond hair pulled up into a messy bun on the top of his head greets me at the door.

"That's me," I respond with an even smile. "I'm Chase, but you can call me Ando if you want."

"I'm Sasha, Gabriel's best friend and the devil on his shoulder," the man tells me.

"I hope that means you're encouraging him to date me and not the other way around."

His blue eyes light up, and he nods. "Absolutely. You are exactly what our boy needs in his life. If you ever need someone to give Gabriel a kick in the pants, I'm your man," he assures me.

I chuckle. "Thank you for your support."

"Ugh... of course you had to answer the door," Gabe grumbles, looking adorable as always.

He's not wearing his go-to outfit I've seen him in—a pair of jeans that could probably fit him better and a plain hoodie. No, today he's got on jeans that perfectly hug his ass and a long sleeve shirt showing off his body instead of hiding it. He looks good enough to eat. *Did he put in extra effort in his outfit today just for me?*

"Of course, I opened the door," Sasha tells Gabe. "Wouldn't want your guy waiting out in the cold."

Gabe rolls his eyes while reaching behind his friend for his coat.

"Did you not want me to meet him?" Sasha inquires with a smirk.

Gabe sighs, clearly frustrated with his friend. "You know it's not that," he mumbles.

"Is the quarterback here?" a man I can't see shouts.

"Yup," Sasha replies. "Get Max down here."

"Oh my god," Gabe mutters, pushing up his glasses to pinch the bridge of his nose.

If I had a smaller ego, I might be nervous that Gabe doesn't want me to meet his friends, but I have enough confidence to power an entire town. He's not ashamed of me. He just doesn't like being the center of attention. I love that his friends don't give a shit, though, and are giving him a gentle push out of his comfort zone. It would be one thing if they completely disregarded his boundaries, but that doesn't seem to be happening.

"Should we make a run for it?" I whisper to Gabe, loving how his face lights up at my suggestion.

"I'd say yes, but they'll only corner you next time. Best to get it out of the way now."

I smile, loving that he's already thinking about a next time because so am I. I've never been the biggest on relationships, just causal flings here and there and more than a few one-night stands, but I could see Gabe being the guy who changes that. Even though we seem like polar opposites to the outside world, we mesh so fucking well. I'm pretty sure I've heard a saying about opposites being good for each other. I just can't remember how it goes.

"He's even hotter in person," says the man who was shouting earlier.

"Stop embarrassing me," Gabe pleads, but the man with dirty blond hair and thick-framed glasses shakes his head.

"What would be the fun in that?" the man teases. "I'm Victor, by the way." He sticks his hand out to me, and I take it.

"Chase, but like I told Sasha, you can call me Ando. Most people do."

"I'm Max," the other man who joined us in the foyer says with a wave. He's on the shorter side of the friend group and has a round face with dark hair.

"It's nice to meet you all," I reply.

"Is this the time that we have the break-his-heart-and-die conversation, or do we wait a couple more dates," Sasha stage whispers to the others, obviously wanting me to hear his words.

Gabe throws his head back, letting out an exasperated sigh. "You're not going to have to have the conversation because you're going to scare him off right now."

I chuckle and reach for Gabe's hand. "It's going to take a lot more to scare me off than a couple of good friends who clearly only want what's best for you," I assure him.

The blush I love creeps up his cheeks, and he nibbles on his lower lip.

"Aww... you landed yourself a heartthrob and a sweet-heart. You're one lucky son of a bitch," Victor teases.

"I hate to cut this short, but I'm kind of hungry," I tell the guys. "How about we plan a night where we can all get together and hang out? I'll even invite my roommates too."

"That sounds fun," Max says, and the other guys nod in agreement.

"Perfect, Gabe and I will try to work out a time that works for everyone."

With those parting words, I pull Gabe out of the house toward my car, giving him a kiss on the cheek once we're outside.

"Sorry about that," he mumbles. "I was expecting something like that to happen, but it still didn't make it any less awkward."

I laugh, shaking my head. "It wasn't a big deal at all. If those are your closest friends, I expect them to give us a hard time for a while. They wouldn't be good friends if they didn't."

His smile grows. "Yeah. They kind of are the best."

This time, I take a chance and open Gabe's door for him. He eyes me up and down but doesn't fight it, so I take it as a win.

"How did you meet them?" I ask once I'm behind the wheel.

"Max and I shared a class together, and he was searching for another roommate. Victor was already living there. Max met Sasha the following year and offered him the final bedroom. The rest is kind of history. We all get along great, which isn't common, but I'm super thankful for it. I've always struggled to make friends. In case you haven't noticed, I'm not the most outgoing guy."

"I'm glad you found your people. They're important to have."

We spend the short drive talking about school and how our classes are going. It's crazy how easy it is to talk to him, especially now that he's letting me in. I still sense he has a bit of a guard around him, but it's slowly coming down.

Arriving at the diner, an older lady sits us at a booth in the back, and we take our time reading the menu.

"Are you a sweet or savory kind of breakfast person?" I ask Gabe, scanning through the items.

"It depends on the day," he responds. "But I'd say I usually lean savory. What about you?"

"If I had the choice, I'd choose sweet every day, but that isn't exactly on the recommended diet for an athlete," I tell him.

"What's it like being a student-athlete?" he questions, his head tilted.

"Stressful at times… our schedules are usually jam-packed. I wouldn't even be here right now if we had an away game. I'd be on a bus or a plane making my way to whatever city we're up against," I explain. "But I love football. It's all I've ever known, and it is what I want to do for as long as I'm able."

"The internet says you're extremely talented," he murmurs.

I can't help but beam at him. "Have you been googling me?"

"Maybe," he murmurs. "But don't let it get to your head. I just wanted to know more about the guy I'm seeing."

"I'm an open book, baby. Ask me anything," I say, holding my hands out in a bring-it-on motion.

Before he can say anything, our waitress comes to take our orders.

Once we're alone, Gabe stares at me silently with an intense gaze. What is going through his head? "Is this just a casual fling, or are you wanting something more?" he eventually asks.

"Being so busy with football, I never loved the idea of having a relationship," I admit. "I was always afraid I would let the person down, so why even start something bound to crash and burn." Gabe's face falls. *Shit, I'm going about this all wrong.* "That was before I met you," I add quickly. "No one felt worth the effort. We both have intense schedules, but I'm willing to put in the effort to try something more with you."

His brows shoot up, and a glimmer of hope passes behind his eyes. "Really?"

I nod. "Yeah. Obviously, I can't tell the future, and I don't know where I'm going to be next year, but I'd like to give us a shot. We can figure out the future when it comes."

"If anyone else would have said those words to me, I'd be running for the hills," Gabe states. "I don't do well with the unknown. I like to have things planned out as much as possible. But you make me want to throw caution to the wind and live in the moment for once."

"So, you aren't afraid that we are completely opposite people anymore?" I inquire.

He shakes his head. "Opposites do attract."

I point at him. "That's it." Gabe looks at me, confused by my sudden outburst. "I'm horrible at remembering common sayings. I've been wracking my brain for that one for the past couple of days," I explain.

He snickers. "That fits you to a T."

"Do you mind that I'm not the smartest guy around?" I ask, a very random burst of insecurity washing over me.

"Do you mind that I'm not a sports guy?" he counters, and I shake my head. "Then you have your answer. Besides, brains aren't everything. Some of the smartest people in the world are also the most evil. A kind heart is much better, and that's something you have without a doubt."

His praise makes me all warm and fuzzy inside. I'm so fucking glad I didn't give up on pursuing him.

Our food arrives much faster than I thought it would, and we both dive in, me a little more quickly than Gabe. His eating habits are a lot like his personality—calm and collected. Me, on the other hand, not so much. I've been scolded a time or two for how fast I shovel in my food.

"So, we have a home game tomorrow. Would you be inter-ested in coming to watch me?" I ask after I've taken a few bites. "You can bring your friends if you don't want to be alone. Also, Rio will be there. He's dying to meet you."

He takes a sip of his water before responding, and I wait with bated breath. "Okay," Gabe answers, making me want to dance around the diner, but I don't. I might be an over-the-top kind of guy, but even I wouldn't make a scene like that. "I'll see if Sasha is available. He's also not a sports guy, but he'll be the easiest to persuade."

"Perfect. I'll let Rio know you're coming."

"Just send me all the information I'll need to know," he requests, and I nod.

"Absolutely. I hope you know you just made me the happiest guy ever right now."

He smirks and shakes his head slowly. "You're easy to make happy."

I shrug, not denying it. "Maybe. But knowing that you're going to a football game *just* for me is next-level kind of happiness."

"You're so lame," he murmurs, but that smirk is still on his lips.

I always play my best, but tomorrow I'm going to try even harder. I'll have someone special watching me after all.

CHAPTER FIFTEEN

Gabriel

FOOTBALL IS AN OUTSIDE SPORT, and we're in Michigan in the wintertime. Why the hell did I agree to come to this game?

Oh, that's right, the quarterback specifically invited me, and it's impossible to say no to his puppy dog eyes. Thankfully, I have all the proper winter gear, so I'm not freezing my toes off.

"Where are we meeting this Rio guy?" Sasha asks as we walk across the parking lot.

"At the doors," I remind him.

"Is he hot too? Is he gay? Would you mind if I hooked up with him?" Sasha rapid-fires the questions.

"I've never met him, so I don't know if he's attractive or gay, but if he is and you want to tap that, I'm not going to stop you," I reply.

Sasha leans his shoulder into mine. "This is why we're best friends."

I chuckle, scanning the area as we get closer to the doors, spotting a guy who looks like Chase described. "Are you Rio?" I ask the man with shaggy blond hair, wearing a GSU Koala jersey and a green beanie.

He smiles at me and nods. "I am. You must be Gabriel."

"That's me, and this is Sasha," I introduce.

"Nice to meet you," Sasha says, holding his hand out and batting his eyes.

Rio chuckles and shakes it. "I've heard a lot about you already."

"I'm flattered. I was unaware I had such a big reputation," Sasha replies flirtatiously.

Rio shakes his head, still grinning, then hands me a jersey. "Chase asked me to give this to you."

I hold it up to see Chase's last name and number on the back.

"Damn, things are getting serious," Sasha muses out loud.

"Will it fit over my coat?" I check, and Rio nods.

"Oh, yeah. He made sure to size up. Most people aren't crazy enough to attend a football game in November without a decent jacket."

I smile and slip the jersey over my head. "How do I look?" I inquire.

"Like you've got a boyfriend who wants to stake a claim on you," Sasha replies, his grin so big it's almost evil-looking. "I approve."

Rio and I laugh, then he guides us into the stadium to apparently the best seats in the place.

"Care to give me a rundown of football?" Sasha asks Rio once we're seated.

Rio starts with what to expect, but I'm not listening that closely. I'm too busy taking in my surroundings. The last time I went to a football game, I was seven. My dad spent most of it yelling at me for not being more excited.

I push away the negative memory, trying to focus on the here and now. I don't let my family have a hold on me anymore. I've worked hard to replace as many bad memories with new, positive ones as possible, and today is another chance to do just that. I'm going to enjoy this moment and forget about my toxic father.

A few of Chase's other friends eventually join us, and this guy everyone calls Coop seems to have caught Sasha's eye.

"Tell me more about hockey," Sasha pleads, batting his lashes again. I shake my head at his antics.

"It's so wild that you guys have been at GSU for this long, and this is your first game," Coop says, shaking his head. "If I tell you more about hockey, will you come to my game tomorrow?" he asks my friend, who nods enthusiastically.

"Is Coop gay?" I whisper to Rio.

"Bi, but he's a player, so if your friend is a relationship kind of guy, I'd get him out now," he warns me.

"Sasha is also a slut, so there are no worries there," I tell him. "I don't think we'll ever see the day that Sasha settles down."

Rio chuckles. "Same with Coop. He's always joking about how he's too wild to be tamed. I pity the fool who falls for him."

"What about you?" I inquire. "Do you like to play the field, or are you a relationship kind of guy?"

"Relationship," he replies quickly. "I'm demisexual, so I have to have a connection with someone before I'm even remotely turned on. I thought I was broken for so long."

"That must be tough."

Rio shrugs. "It was before I knew what it was. Now, I've just come to accept it. It does make dating in college a lot harder since most people are looking for a quick *wham bam, thank you, ma'am*. Thankfully, soccer keeps me busy."

People around us start to yell when the cheerleaders and a giant Koala mascot make their way onto the field.

"Is Chase bi?" I whisper to Rio as the gorgeous women and a few men dance around.

Rio laughs and shakes his head. "He's gay, and even if he were bi, he only has eyes for you. You have nothing to worry about."

Heat rushes to my face and the tops of my ears at his

words. I've never felt so wanted by someone before. The fact that Chase is talking about me to his friends says a lot.

The cheerleaders are done with their short routine, and the football team comes out, the crowd so loud it's almost deafening. An excited buzz of energy fills the air, making me almost lightheaded.

"There's your man," Rio elbows me, pointing to number twelve on the field.

Chase scans the bleachers, and when his eyes land on me, he waves like a maniac, causing me to blush even harder. Never in a million years did I think I would be dating a quarterback, but here we are.

The game starts, and the crowd settles a bit, but people still yell and cheer at random moments. I'm having a hard time following everything since the game seems to be going too fast, but despite feeling a bit lost, I am having a good time anyway. Maybe it's because I'm surrounded by a great group of people who are treating me like an equal even though I'm completely out of my element.

When the Koalas score their first touchdown, I join in with the crowd yelling and clapping.

"You look really happy right now," Sasha tells me when the game is at halftime.

"I'm having a great time," I reply with a big grin. "I know people say that you have to experience a game in real life to understand what's so addictive about sports, but I've been to more than one game, and they all sucked. I'm figuring out that it's not just about going to a live game, but about the people you surround yourself with."

Sasha nods. "I'm having a blast too…" He pauses, then leans in to whisper, "I'm really hoping that Coop will take me home tonight and rearrange my insides."

I bark out a laugh before turning my attention back to the game, which goes by faster than I expected. It's a nail-biting finish, but the Koalas take home the win.

"Ready to go?" Rio asks when people start filing out, and Sasha leaves with Coop, to no one's surprise.

I nod and follow him to his car. I got someone to cover my shift tonight, and Chase asked me if I would feel comfortable spending the night. I'm a bit nervous but also beyond excited.

"How long will it take Chase to get home?" I check with Rio once we're inside the already warm vehicle. Remote start is a thing of dreams.

Rio tips his head from side to side. "It depends. Could be anywhere from thirty minutes to two hours. But knowing him, he'll be home as fast as possible," he assures me. "Want to watch a movie and eat pizza while we wait? I'm beyond excited to have more flexibility in my diet for the next little while, and I've been craving the cheesy greasiness."

I laugh but also feel bad that his soccer team was knocked out of the championships in round one. "I'll help you devour a pie."

"Perfect," he replies with a toothy grin.

If someone had told me a month ago that I would be hanging out with athletes and dating a quarterback, I would have had them committed because, clearly, they were insane.

It turns out I was the one in the wrong, and this is my life now, at least for the time being.

CHAPTER SIXTEEN

Chase

MY PERMANENT SMILE as I enter my apartment only grows when I find Gabe chilling on the couch with my best friend. I'm still riding on the high from our win, but an extra jolt of excitement rushes through my veins at the sight of the smile on my guy's face.

"You've got to be kidding me," Gabe says to Rio. They are both so enthralled in the story that neither hears me enter.

"Nope, the dare was just to run through the hall naked, but Chase has always been one to up the ante," Rio tells him, and I chuckle at the memory.

People learned quickly not to dare me to do anything after I helicoptered my dick in front of the teacher's lounge. I was suspended for that stunt, but it was totally worth it. I'm honestly surprised it didn't earn me a better nickname, but what exactly would it be? Calling me Helicopter would be weird. Dare Devil would have been a cool nickname, but it's too long. I guess that's why they stuck with Ando.

"We all knew people were going to see my dick. I just gave them an extra show." Both of the guys jump at my response, and I can't help but laugh. When Rio glares at me, I lift my hands in surrender. "Hey, don't give me those dagger eyes. I'm not the one who was so into the story he was telling that he didn't hear his roommate getting home."

Rio rolls his eyes, but Gabe chuckles. The sound fills me with warmth. Damn, I'm really into this guy.

"It was a great story. It's hard not to get lost in it," Gabe defends himself and my friend.

"Did you eat already?" I check with them, and they nod.

"We had a giant greasy pizza. It was amazing," Rio moans the words out.

"It's not nice to tease me like that," I scold him teasingly. "I'm not off my athlete diet yet. We only have one game left of our regular season, but if all goes according to plan, we'll be playing another five games after that and bringing home the championship. So, all I got for supper was chicken, veg, and rice."

"You don't ever cheat?" Gabe asks.

"Oh, I do. I just know I'll feel like a bag of shit tomorrow if I do. Some things are worth cheating over, though."

"He'll never turn down a piece of chocolate cheesecake," Rio informs him.

"I would die for chocolate cheesecake," I tell him solemnly.

"Noted," he responds with a smirk.

I head to my room quickly to drop off my bag, double-checking that it's neat and tidy. Yes, Gabe has already seen it once, but I don't need him thinking I'm some slob.

When I return, the guys are watching a show I've never seen before, but it seems cool, even if it also looks old. "What are you watching?" I inquire, plopping myself on the couch as close to Gabe as possible without crushing him.

"*Doctor Who,*" he replies with a big grin.

I wrap my arm around his shoulder, and he instantly leans into me. He feels so fucking good in my arms, like this is exactly where he's meant to be. Like he was made to be with me. No one I've ever dated before felt this right.

"What is that?" I ask.

Gabe throws his head back and groans. "I know you guys are jocks, but how have neither of you heard of *Doctor Who?*"

"I'm actually pissed I didn't know about it sooner. This show is the bomb," Rio says.

I shrug. "You know me, I'll try anything once. Bring on the doctor show."

Gabe and Rio laugh, and we fall into a comfortable silence while watching the show.

By the end of the episode, I'm hooked and plead with Rio not to skip ahead of me. We are going to have to plan out many nights to watch the show. Apparently, it has thirty-nine seasons, and the first episode aired in 1963. Gabe said there are around nine hundred episodes for us to watch, which is insane, but I'm here for it. Bring on the binge-a-thon.

I fake a yawn as the credits finish playing, and Gabe lifts his chin to look at me.

"Tired already?" he checks.

"Maybe a little. Want to cuddle in my room?"

"Just say you want some alone time to be naked with your boyfriend," Rio teases. "You don't have to make up some lame excuse about being tired."

"What if I really *am* tired?" I counter.

"I've known you for over two years. You are never tired this early."

I could argue with him, but what would be the point? He isn't wrong. So, I grab Gabe's hand and pull him to my room.

"Have fun!" Rio shouts before I can shut the door.

When I look at Gabe, he has a weird look on his face that I can't decipher. His cheeks are pink, which is normal for him, but his brows are pulled together, and he looks confused.

"What's up?" I check.

He slowly shakes his head and looks at the floor. "It's nothing."

"You know you don't have to hide from me, right? Did I say something wrong? Was I being too presumptuous? If you don't tell me, I'm going to be running through every worst-case scenario in my head."

A tiny smile pulls at his lips, and he finally meets my eyes. "It's just that Rio called me your boyfriend."

"Did you not like it?" I ask. *Am I seeing us as something more than he is?*

He shakes his head again. "No, I did like it, but I was a little shocked you didn't say anything to him."

I place my hand on his cheek and stroke it with my thumb. "I like you, Gabe, maybe more than I should for only knowing you for less than a month. I don't mind people calling you my boyfriend. I actually like the title as long you're okay with it. I know we've only been on two dates, but I don't see me wanting to let you go any time soon."

Gabe nibbles on his lower lip, staring into my eyes with this intense energy as if he's trying to figure out whether I'm telling the truth. "I'm okay with it," he eventually whispers.

A giant smile grows on my face, and I pull Gabe toward me, slanting my lips over his. He melts into me immediately, making my heart beat a little faster. Has anyone been so pliant with me before?

I keep one hand on his face while the other finds purchase on his hip, pulling him even tighter to me, not wanting any space between us. Gabe's hands lift to my neck, his fingers caressing my skin, and his touch sends tingles of need throughout my entire body, but I'm not ready to rush into bed with him yet. I want to enjoy this moment for just a little bit longer.

Gabe's tongue licks at the seam of my lips after a few simple kisses, and I gladly open for him, humming as his tongue laps at mine.

"You're a good kisser," Gabe tells me when we break for air.

I chuckle. "You're not so bad yourself. Ready for some cuddling?" I wink, and he laughs.

"Depends what kind of cuddling you have in mind," he replies with a sexy smirk.

I push my hips into his so he can feel how hard I am. "What kind do you want?"

He waggles his brows, then grabs my crotch. "This fun kind."

I groan as the touch sends jolts of lust throughout my body. "Seems like we're on the same page. Now strip. I want to taste you."

He laughs but obeys my command. I take a moment to watch him before stripping out of my clothes. He's so fucking hot that it has me throbbing, but it's also more than that. He's kind, odd, and different from anyone I've ever been with. This isn't a casual fling for me, but how long will I actually be able to make this last?

Gabe wasn't wrong to be nervous about us coming from two different worlds, but I'm too selfish to let him go now that I have him.

CHAPTER SEVENTEEN

CHASE STARES at me with the same intensity he did the first time he saw me naked. The weight of his gaze makes me shiver a little.

"You're fucking gorgeous," he murmurs, and I blush, something I can't seem to stop, especially around Chase. I used to be super self-conscious about blushing as easily as I do. He doesn't make fun of me for it, and it's almost as if he likes it.

Taking a brave step forward, I place my hand on his chest. "You're pretty sexy yourself," I reply while allowing my fingers to trail down his torso, dancing through his treasure trail, following the path to the prize they are searching for.

When my fingers finally arrive at his hard cock, I wrap them around him and give a gentle yet firm squeeze.

"Jesus," he pants out, causing the corners of my lips to turn upward.

Dropping to my knees, I stare up at him, loving the way his eyes darken when I lick at the slit of his leaking dick. "Mm…" I hum in appreciation, then lap at his crown. "You taste so fucking good, and I love how much you leak."

I've never been a guy who leaks that much precum, but I love that Chase is. The salty and tangy yet oddly sweet taste coats my tongue, and I suck him into my mouth so I can savor the flavor some more. Humming around his length, I bob up and down, eliciting deep, guttural moans from the hot-as-sin quarterback. His hands fall to my head, and I'm desperate for him to take control and fuck my face, but I doubt he's going to do that unless I give him permission, so I pull back with an audible pop, the sound loud in the otherwise quiet room, and stare up at him.

"Will you fuck my face?" I request, which earns me a lust-filled growl.

"You have no idea how badly I want to do that, but I was also wondering if you wanted to try something more."

I bite my lip and tilt my head to the side. "What do you have in mind?"

"I want to play with your ass. Can I finger fuck you while you suck my cock?" he requests. "That is if you're into anal play. I'm okay if you're not. There are other ways we can get off together."

I chuckle while caressing his thigh. "I'm into anal play. I'm also a strict bottom, if that's okay with you?"

Chase's smile grows, and he nods. "I think I'm vers, but I prefer to top."

"Looks like we are a perfect match then," I reply.

"And you thought we wouldn't have anything in common," he teases, stepping away from me.

He opens his nightstand drawer and pulls out a bottle of lube before sitting on the edge of his bed and tilting his head at me. "Come here, gorgeous."

I crawl to him, not missing the way his breath hitches. A look of lust heats his face as his eyes track my every movement. "*Fuck...* you look so hot right now," he whispers in a raspy voice.

When I'm between his legs, he grips my chin and pulls me up for a toe-curling kiss before gently removing my glasses and setting them on the nightstand. As he's putting my glasses away, I get back into position and lap at his cock from root to tip. "Show me how talented those fingers are," I tell him before opening my mouth and swallowing him down my throat.

"Holy shit," he mutters.

The click of the cap on the bottle of lube fills my ears. I can't help but wiggle my ass in the air in anticipation.

"Are you needy for me, baby?" he inquires, and I nod without letting him out of my mouth.

Chase leans over me, the new position, pressing him further into my mouth and burying my face in his pelvis. My lack of a gag reflex allows me to swallow around him, relishing the groan it pulls from him.

A moment later, a slippery finger starts to circle my pucker. "So fucking beautiful," he whispers, then slowly slips his digit inside me. I moan around him as he gently slides his finger in and out of my tight channel. It's been a while since I've played with myself and even longer since I've been with an actual partner. I'm kind of glad that Chase didn't suggest we jump right into him fucking me tonight. I want that eventually, but I'd like to work up to it. He isn't a small guy, and I don't want to get hurt.

While I continue to bob up and down on Chase's perfect dick, he slides in a second finger, and my eyes roll into the back of my head. *Fuck, it feels sooo good.*

"Still want me to fuck your face, baby?" he asks, panting just as heavily as I am. I nod, desperate for him to use me. "Tap my leg if it gets too much. You're so fucking perfect," he praises before bucking his hips and lodging his cock deep into the back of my throat. I swallow around him, and he lets out a deep, guttural groan.

I love being able to make him sound like that.

Chase fucks my face like I requested, using my throat for his pleasure. It makes me a little lightheaded but in the best possible way. Each time he hits the back of my throat, I swallow, allowing the muscles to constrict around him, enjoying the way he groans. Every once in a while, he slows his punishing thrusts, allowing me to take control so I can breathe briefly before taking back the reins and owning me. It's the best thing ever.

"I'm fucking close, baby," he tells me, angling his now three fingers inside me to probe my prostate, causing me to cry out. "You can stroke yourself if you need to, but I'd really like you to come in my mouth after." His voice is husky as he makes the request, and I know that's exactly what I want.

I don't bother telling him I'm in complete agreement. I simply keep sucking, desperate for his release. At that moment, he loses his control, fucking my face with everything he has. His fingers slow while he focuses on his impending orgasm, but I don't mind. I love how he's acting like a caveman and giving me everything he has.

Chase bites his knuckle, his hips jerking in short, deep thrusts when he comes down my throat, trying to cover the roar that rips past his lips. With his free hand, he presses the back of my head into him, making it hard to breathe, but I don't care as I swallow everything he gives me with a heady feeling that I was able to make him come so hard.

Once he's spent, he slides out of me, pulling his finger from my ass at the same time, leaving me feeling a little empty and missing the connection. Then, with shaky hands, he lifts me, sets me on the bed, and switches places with me. "Time to give me that load," he states, then takes me into his hot, wet mouth.

He's quick to hollow his cheeks, suctioning me between his needy lips, causing me to gasp. "Fuck," I breathe out, and it's hard to tell without my glasses, but I'm pretty sure Chase is smiling at me.

After being thoroughly finger-fucked, I was already close to my release, and now that Chase is sucking me like a kid with a lollipop, I know I'm not going to be able to hold it back.

Chase stops for a moment and pushes me to lie on my

back while helping me raise my legs. "Time to give me every last drop, gorgeous," he instructs, engulfing me again.

This time, he slides a finger back inside me, and the moment he strokes against my prostate, I cry out, forgetting to cover my shout as I explode with an overwhelmingly intense orgasm. Like Chase promised, he devours every last drop, and I'm entirely spent when he comes up for air.

"I hope your roommates don't give me a hard time about being loud." I blush when Chase climbs on the bed with me and pulls me into his arms.

He kisses my shoulder and shrugs. "If they do, I'll just make sure my next prank on them is a doozy."

"What kind of pranks do you play on them?" I ask, my fingers lazily dancing across his stomach.

"Ice down their boxers to wake them up, putting salt in the sugar bowl, tying their laces together. Dumb shit like that," he lists off.

I shake my head against his chest. "Doesn't that get old?"

"Not even a little," he replies, and even though I'm not looking at his face, I can tell he's grinning from ear to ear. "But the payback kind of sucks."

"If you can't take the heat, stay out of the kitchen," I tell him.

"What do pranks have to do with cooking?" he questions, and I chuckle.

"It's just a figure of speech."

Chase hums, but it sounds sleepy. I turn my head to look at him, and his eyes are slowly shutting. "Goodnight, handsome," I whisper and kiss his chest.

"Goodnight, gorgeous," he replies, pressing a kiss to the top of my head, turning me into a puddle of goo.

Maybe things would be easier if Chase wasn't so sweet.

How am I ever going to say goodbye when he treats me so special?

CHAPTER EIGHTEEN

Chase

ONE WEEK LATER

OUR REGULAR FOOTBALL season ended last night, and we went out with a bang. Literally. Hendo took 'go hard' a little too literally and ended up blowing out his knee. It was hard for all of us to witness. There's a strong possibility his football career will be over before it even has a chance to start. I feel so bad for the guy, but I've still got to keep my head in the game.

Even with Hendo's injury, we were able to keep our winning streak. Now we have to focus on making it through the rounds of the championship so we can bring home the big W. I'm determined to do it for Hendo and Rio. I still hate that his soccer team bombed in the first round, but shit happens.

"How is Brett doing?" Gabe asks when I meet him at the coffee shop.

"His spirits are in the gutter, but physically, he's okay," I tell my cute and nerdy boyfriend. "He'll be in the hospital for a couple of days, then he's going home. His mom is a physical therapist, so she'll be able to help with his recovery."

"Is he going to be able to play football again?" Gabe inquires.

I blow out a breath and shrug. "Only time will tell, but an

injury like that is usually enough to stop someone from ever going pro."

Gabe's face falls, and I feel the same amount of sadness. "Poor guy," he whispers.

I nod. "I don't know what I'd do if I were in his shoes. Football is my life, and Hendo is a lot like me."

"I'm sure he'll find another path forward, just like you would if you were in that boat," he assures me.

He means well by his words, but I don't see any other path forward. Sure, I'm getting a degree in business, but what would I actually do with it? Football has always been my one goal in life, and I don't know how I would be able to give it up.

"How are your grades coming along?" Gabe asks, bringing the conversation back to where it should be, and it brings a smile to my lips.

If you had told me a month ago that I would be happy with this class, I would have said you were crazy, but that's exactly where I am. With Gabe's help, I've been able to gain an understanding of the class and turn my grades around in roughly three weeks. I didn't think it was possible when I first met him. Now, I would have to do something really stupid to fail, and there is no way that is going to happen.

"Fucking amazing," I tell him with my chin held high. "We've only got like one week left of classes, and my grade is well above passing."

Gabe's face lights up. "I'm so proud of you."

"None of this would have been possible without you, babe. You got me to understand something that felt alien to me. I'm forever going to be in your debt."

My sexy nerd rolls his eyes at my sappiness and shakes his head. "I may have given you a helping hand, but you're the one who has put in the hard work. Now, you just need to keep it up so you can finish this semester strong."

"What are your plans for Christmas this year?" I ask him while we are studying.

"The usual, hanging out with Nana," he says, keeping his nose in his book.

"Do you think you'd want to spend Christmas with me this year? Your nana could come too," I add so that he doesn't think I'm trying to keep him away from his family.

He freezes, his eyes still fixed downward, but finally, he lifts his gaze to meet mine, looking shocked at my request.

"You want me to meet your family?" he checks, and I nod.

"By then, we'll have been dating for over a month, but I hope you know I'm already crazy about you, even if it has only been not quite two weeks."

A small smile spreads across his lips, and his cheeks turn that color I adore so much.

"I'll talk to Nana about it and see what she thinks," he says, and I fist-bump the air, not even caring that people are watching me make a fool of myself. "You're an idiot, albeit an adorable idiot." Gabe's words are hushed, but the smile on his lips tells me he's teasing.

This playful side of him is something I could become addicted to.

Approximately Three Weeks Later

To say I was beyond excited when Gabe told me he could come to Christmas with my family was an understatement. I literally jumped around my room like a teenage girl. I'm not ashamed to admit that, either.

"Are you sure your nana doesn't want to come?" I ask Gabe for the millionth time, and he nods.

"Apparently, she's going to spend Christmas with her best friend and build more puzzles," he reminds me. "I don't see the joy in that, but I won't force her to do something she doesn't want to do either. But she did make me promise that we'll spend New Year's with her."

"Works for me. But do you think she'll bake me a cake?" I ask.

"Why would she bake you a cake?" he counters, his brows scrunched together in an adorable way.

"Because it's my birthday," I tell him with a bright grin.

"It is? Why didn't you tell me? I bet you have better things to do than hang out with me and my nana for your twenty-first birthday."

I shake my head and stare intently into his eyes. "There is no one I'd rather spend that day with than you. Besides, I can plan a separate party with my friends any day. They are always looking for an excuse to let loose."

The way his face lights up at my words assures me I'm making the right decision.

"So, as soon as my game is finished on Saturday, we are going to drive straight to my parents' house," I remind him.

"Sounds good to me. Make sure you play your heart out. I want to see you win."

My face hurts from how big I'm smiling, but it feels damn good to have my boyfriend cheering me on. "I plan on it."

None of us are taking any of these games lightly. Saturday is the semifinals. If we win, we'll be heading for the championship game. Scratch the if. It's *when* we win because I don't plan on letting the other team take this away from us.

I still can't believe Christmas is almost here, and the semester is behind us. I thought I would be spending these weeks crying in my pillow because I failed my class, but I'm not. I'm running off the high of winning game after game and hopefully winning the heart of the adorable nerd who has definitely stolen mine.

We've been dating for five weeks now, and I'm already head over heels for him. I think he feels the same way, but sometimes it's hard to tell. Neither of us has said the four-letter word that starts with L yet, but I plan on changing that on Christmas.

Because I do love him.

CHAPTER NINETEEN

TODAY, I'm meeting Chase's family for the first time, and saying I am a little nervous would be an understatement. I wish Nana had come along, but I understand why she turned down the invitation. She really did have plans with her best friend, but she also has a bad hip, making traveling uncomfortable. At least we'll be able to spend New Year's with her. And she totally agreed to bake Chase a cake. A chocolate cheesecake, if we're being precise here.

He still has one football game to play in the new year, but I don't think one or two pieces of cake will cost him the win.

"They're going to love you," Chase tells me, squeezing my leg while he drives us to the house he grew up in.

"How can you be so certain?" I ask, staring out the window at everything covered in snow.

"Because you're kind of hard not to love," he whispers.

I gasp and stare at him.

Did he just say what I think he said?

He chuckles and shakes his head. "I was planning on saying this more romantically, but if you didn't pick up on that... I love you, Gabe. You turned my world upside down and changed it for the better."

"I never in a million years thought I'd be dating a quarterback, let alone falling for one, but I love you too. Even if you are a weirdo who likes sports," I tell him.

"Admit it, football's growing on you too," he says, giving me a gentle nudge.

"I will admit no such thing," I reply, tilting my chin up in defiance.

Chase chuckles. "You're cute when you lie."

The rest of the drive flies by in a blur as we chat about nothing and everything and even sing along to the radio from time to time. I've never been so at ease around someone I've dated. I guess that just means I wasn't dating the right person. This is what a relationship should be like. I hope we can hold on to this for the long run because if something tears us apart, it's going to be one hell of a heartbreak.

By the time we arrive at the Anderson household, it's late, and I'm tired, but that doesn't lessen my anxiety at all. This is my first time meeting someone's parents, and I'm desperate to make a good impression.

"You made it!" a beautiful woman with light brown hair and eyes that match Chase's calls out as we're unloading our suitcases from the back of the car.

"Told you we'd be here," Chase tells whom I'm assuming is his mom.

"You undersold just how handsome your boyfriend is," she tells Chase while eyeing me with a warm smile. "I'm Hannah. It's so nice to meet you, Gabriel."

"It's nice to meet you," I mutter, sticking my hand out, but she doesn't take it.

"Do you mind if we hug?" she asks, and I love that she's not just assuming that's something I'm going to enjoy.

"Okay," I whisper, letting her pull me into her arms.

Just like her son, Hannah gives the best hugs, and I melt into her. My own mother never hugged me like this, and it's really fucking nice. I hold onto her for a while, then realize tears are trickling down my face. I'm not necessarily sad. I just hate that I had the parents I did. Younger me didn't deserve to have cold parents who hated his very existence.

"Are you okay?" Chase asks when I let his mom go and wipe my face.

"Sorry. I've just never had a mom hug like that before... it was nice."

Hannah smiles at me in that soft, motherly way Nana often looks at me. "If you ever need another one, I'm here. I'll never turn down a hug."

I thank her, then follow the two of them into the house.

"Chase is home," Hannah yells once we've closed the door, and feet thunder down the hall before three younger people join us, followed by a tall man who looks like an older version of Chase. He's handsome. At least I know now that Chase is going to age well.

"These three rug rats are my brother, Henry, and my sisters, Isla and Marigold," Chase introduces.

"Yes, I got the old lady name, but I'm the prettiest," the youngest of the Anderson siblings says with a boatload of attitude.

"Excuse me, did you forget about my existence?" Isla argues.

"I'm pretty sure I'm the prettiest," Henry teases his sisters.

"I'm Oliver," Chase's dad says, reaching his hand out to me. "It's a pleasure to meet you, Gabriel. Please make yourself at home and excuse my children for their lack of manners. I tried to raise them well, but clearly, I failed."

I chuckle while shaking his hand. "It's all good. The banter is actually entertaining," I admit.

"Just wait until the girls start fighting over a boy they like," Chase whispers. "It's not so entertaining then, but I'll protect you from them. We can always sneak away if they're getting too much."

"Barf." Marigold puts her finger in her mouth like she's about to gag.

"Okay, give the poor boys some space," Hannah calls out, shooing her children away. "Why don't you two go and unpack, then come down for a snack? We don't have much planned for tonight, so feel free to relax."

I follow Chase up the stairs to his room, and he puts our suitcases in the closet. "How are you doing?" he checks while moving to sit on the bed and patting the spot beside him.

I join him, leaning my head on his shoulder. "Not bad. Your family is nice. I'm just not used to everyone being so in your face. Obviously, my family was never like that."

"If you ever need a break, please let me know, and I'll make sure to sneak you away. Tomorrow, we'll make ginger-bread houses, go tobogganing, and watch movies in our Christmas pajamas. On Christmas morning, we'll wake up at the ass crack of dawn to open presents, but there will be time to have a nap before dinner," he tells me, and I smile at him.

"Are you happy to be home?" I inquire, and he nods.

"Family has always been important to me. I really hope I get drafted so I can repay my parents for all they've done for me."

"I'm pretty sure your parents don't want you to repay them. Good parents love and support their children. They don't care about what they get in return as long as their children are decent human beings."

He puts his arm around me and holds me for a minute. "I know they aren't expecting anything out of me, but I want to all the same."

"Do you have a team you want to be signed to the most?" I ask.

"Michigan Raptors is my number one pick, but I'd be content anywhere."

I nod, not sure what else to say. If he gets drafted by Michigan, at least we'll be close, and there is a chance we can make things work, but if he goes halfway across the country, I don't see how a relationship will be possible. I'm aware people make long-distance work, but it's difficult, and I'm positive my insecurities would rear their ugly little heads and eat at me.

"Ready for a snack?" Chase asks after a couple of minutes.

My stomach chooses that moment to grumble, and I laugh. "I guess I could eat."

Chase smiles and stands, offering me his hand, and as my hand settles in his, I realize I love how much he touches me. It's not something I would have said I wanted in the past from a boyfriend, but now it's something I crave.

I just crave *him*.

I hope I can have him for as long as possible.

CHAPTER TWENTY

Chase

"MERRY CHRISTMAS EVE," Marigold cheers when we enter the kitchen.

"She's one of those evil morning people," I whisper to Gabe, who chuckles.

"I'm not evil," Marigold defends. "It's not my fault you can't function without drugs."

"Coffee is not a drug," I growl out at her.

"He's right. It's a necessity," Gabe backs me.

"Google it," Marigold says with a shrug. "Caffeine *is* a drug. You're all just a bunch of drug addicts." She sticks her tongue out at us before skipping out of the kitchen.

"Honestly, I'm fine being this kind of drug addict," I tell Gabe, pouring each of us a cup of coffee, thankful Mom pre-set the machine last night.

He nods, taking the cup from me to doctor it to his liking.

Once we both have coffee in hand, we move to sit at the kitchen table and wait for everyone else to wake up.

"Sorry I couldn't sleep in this morning," Gabe murmurs into his mug. "My body is still on college time. Which isn't the worst thing since Christmas break will fly by, and I'll have to get back on this schedule again before I know it."

"It's not a problem. I like spending time with you."

He smiles and nods before taking another sip of his coffee.

"Please, someone tell me there is coffee," Isla complains as she shuffles into the kitchen.

"It's in the pot, but we're probably going to have to make more soon," I inform her.

"I don't care as long as I can have one cup to start," she says, walking like a zombie to the machine.

"Marigold is the only morning person out of us," I explain to Gabe as he watches my sister.

"I'm still pretty sure she was adopted or at least the spawn of an alien," Isla supplies.

"If she didn't look *just* like you and your mom, you might get away with the adoption allegation," Gabe counters, making her giggle.

"Touché," she replies, pointing at him like he made an excellent point.

"Shall we go with the alien spawn then?" I ask.

"Are you calling your sister an alien again?" Mom inquires, entering the kitchen with a little bit more vigor than Isla but still looking dead on her feet.

"If the probe fits," Isla says, making us all laugh.

Mom pours a cup of coffee for herself, then pours the rest into a travel thermos to keep warm so she can start another pot.

"Are you enjoying yourself so far?" Mom checks with Gabe when she joins us.

"So far, it's been a great visit," he tells her with a genuine smile.

"I'm glad," she replies, beaming at him. "If you need anything, please let me know. I want you to feel like this is your home too."

"Is it sad to say this already feels more like home than my parents' house ever did?" he asks her quietly.

With how my mom's face flinches the tiniest amount, it's obvious to me that Gabe's words are breaking her heart, but she does a good job of covering it up and not clueing him into how she's affected.

"Of course not. I'm so sorry you had to go through that." She places her hand on Gabe's, and he stares at it for a minute. "Just know that you are loved and welcome here."

He offers her the slightest smile. "Could I have another one of those mom hugs?" he requests, and she moves in to wrap her arms around him without missing a beat.

Seeing him so at ease with my family warms my heart, but it also makes me slightly murderous. How dare his family hurt him so deeply. The two people who are supposed to love you unconditionally from the day you are born until the day you die are your parents, and his didn't do that. I know there is a special place in hell for people like them.

"Now, who's ready for some breakfast?" Mom asks, and we all shoot up our hands. She shakes her head with a big smile. "I'll make lots."

While Mom cooks, the rest of us sit at the table, catching up on things we've missed over the past few months. We laugh a ton, and it feels so good it makes me want to pray to whichever deity will listen to grant me a draft from Michigan.

I already miss my family like crazy just being away at school. I don't want to move even farther away from them. I also don't want to move away from Gabe. Maybe I could talk him into following me once he graduates, but that would mean leaving him behind for a year. That option isn't ideal. I could go a few days without seeing him. We already do that. But months? I don't think my heart could take that kind of distance. Or my dick if I'm being honest.

"We're going to start gingerbread houses in about an hour," Mom tells us as we're cleaning up. "And, Marigold, I want you to participate! No more holing up in your room all alone. You know what Christmas means to this family."

Marigold sighs dramatically but nods. "Whatever," she grumbles under her breath while walking out of the kitchen.

"How come the youngest is always the most mouthy?" Dad asks with a look of pure confusion on his face.

"Probably because they learn it from the older siblings," I tell him, and he sighs.

"So, what you're saying is I'm fucked since she had you three as role models?"

I laugh but nod and pat him on the shoulder. "Sorry, old man, but you're going to have your hands full with that one, and you've still got four more years before she goes off to college."

He groans. "Don't remind me."

"Do you mind if I sneak away to have a shower?" Gabe asks.

"Let me show you where everything is," I insist, although I have ulterior motives for helping him.

Once he grabs a change of clothes, I show him to the bathroom, locking the door behind me.

"We can't have shower sex," Gabe whispers, and I shrug.

"We're just conserving water, baby. My parents should be thanking me," I tell him, taking small steps toward him, bringing a hand to his face, and leaning in for a kiss.

"I'll never be able to show my face without being the shade of a tomato," he argues.

I pout as I step back. "Is this a hard pass for you?" I question, and he nods with a frown.

"For now, anyway. Maybe one day I'll be more adventurous. I'm sorry."

I shake my head. "No. You don't have any reason to be sorry. I promise I'll always respect your boundaries. But know that the moment I get you alone in my bedroom again, I'm fucking your brains out."

He laughs, and I let myself out of the bathroom before I can't control myself any longer. I head straight to my room to take a couple of deep breaths and get my throbbing cock under control. I don't need my family to see how horny I am for my boyfriend right now. I consider jerking off but decide better of it since I won't be able to clean up after with Gabe in the bathroom. So, I sit on my bed and focus on breathing and recalling legal terminology from my class. Thankfully, it doesn't take long for my dick to deflate and my heart to stop racing.

It's crazy what Gabe does to me, but I wouldn't change anything.

CHAPTER TWENTY-ONE

CHASE'S FAMILY is the nicest group of people I've ever met, and I'm a little sad when we have to say goodbye. I'm actually going to miss them, especially Hannah. I've never met someone who is so easy to talk to. She actually cared what I had to say. Besides my friends and Nana, I've never really had anyone like that until Chase.

"Don't be a stranger," Hannah tells me, giving me one last bear hug.

"I won't," I promise her.

Chase loads up our bags, and after a few more hugs and goodbyes, we're on our way back to Green Spring.

"I told you they would love you," Chase says.

I nod with an easy smile. "And you were right."

"What did *you* think about them?"

"They're amazing," I tell him with a big grin. "I love how welcoming they are. Your siblings are also hilarious. I haven't laughed that hard in a long time."

"They're the best."

The drive feels shorter on the way home, and maybe it's because I don't have this weight of anxiety in my chest this time.

"Would you like to spend the night with me?" Chase asks as we pass the '*Welcome to Green Spring*' sign. "Rio isn't due back until tomorrow, and Hendo is with his family until who knows when."

"So, we'd have the whole place to ourselves?" I inquire.

"Just you and me, baby." He winks at me. "So, you can be as loud as you want."

My cheeks heat, and my cock hardens in my pants.

"Let me text the guys so they're not worried when I don't show up," I tell him. "Don't need them sending out a search party."

He chuckles. "It really would be a mood killer to have the cops show up when I'm balls deep inside you."

I laugh, but it's huskier than normal. My cock is now painfully hard as I send off the text, letting my friends know where I'll be and that I won't be responding to any messages until tomorrow. Once the message is sent, I put my phone on silent and pocket it.

"I'm all yours for twenty-four hours," I tell him. "Anything you can think of to pass the time?"

The smile he offers me is damn near devilish. "I have a few ideas up my sleeve."

"Then take me home, handsome, and let it be known I expect to be *thoroughly* entertained," I state, making him laugh.

"I'll make sure not to disappoint you," he assures me.

When we arrive at his apartment, the instant our bags hit the floor, Chase has me in his arms, smashing his lips to mine.

"I've wanted you so fucking badly these past couple of days," he says against my lips. "Next time, we should book a hotel room."

I chuckle at the insane idea. "There is no way your parents would allow that."

"You're not wrong. Maybe I'll just have to teach you to be quiet so I don't have to go so long without your body again."

I smile at him and shrug. "We'll see. Now, I was promised entertainment. Show me what you got, big boy," I goad him.

He growls, smashing his lips to mine again. His tongue immediately spears between my lips, dancing with mine. He pushes me up against the wall, thrusting his hips forward, his hard cock pressing into me. I let out a groan of desire and thrust my hips into his leg.

"Do you feel what you do to me, baby?" he asks, breaking the kiss and nipping at my neck.

"The same thing you do to me," I reply breathlessly.

"I need to be inside you, baby," he pleads.

"Then take me," I tell him, devouring him with a kiss.

His hands grip my ass tightly, and he hoists me into his arms. My legs instantly wrap around his torso, and I gasp when he thrusts against me.

"Fuck, I can't even think straight right now. If I had supplies, I'd fuck you up against this wall. I'd have you screaming and panting for me this instant." He growls and nips at my neck, causing my cock to throb in the confines of my pants.

"Too many clothes," I murmur breathlessly.

Chase laps at my neck, then nods and sets me down, grabbing my hand as soon as my feet touch the floor.

"Let's go to my room. That way, as soon as we're naked, I can have you."

I follow him, practically running to keep up with him. *Damn these short legs.*

As soon as we are in his room, his hands and mouth are on me again, and we start to strip out of our clothes.

We kick out of our shoes at the same time and while we undress, I stumble several times since my brain is foggy with desire. I need to have him inside me *now*.

We've talked about it a bunch of times, but the moment hasn't felt right. And with Chase having been gone so much for football, there hasn't really been time. So, we've mostly stuck to blowjobs, hand jobs, and frotting. Now, there is no rush, and we can take our time and do whatever the hell we want.

And I want…

… no, I *need* him inside me tonight.

I'm desperate to have his cock throbbing inside my tight channel as he fucks me so hard it makes me forget my own name. I've never wanted anyone as badly as I want Chase.

We are a fumbling mess as we rid ourselves of our clothes, both of us desperate to be naked as soon as possible, but at the same time, we don't want to stop kissing or groping each other, making things more challenging than they would normally be. With Chase's help, I'm the first one naked, my clothes lying in a pile on the floor. Needing Chase to be, I fumble with his jeans button while he lifts his hand behind his head to pull his shirt off. My fingers are shaky, and it takes me a bit longer to get it open, but as soon as it pops free, I work the fly down, then grab the waistband of his jeans and boxers, pushing them down at the same time. Chase shimmies his hips for me and kicks out of the clothes the instant they hit his ankles. With balance I'm not sure I would possess at this moment, he lifts a foot to remove his sock, then does the same with the other.

We're both naked, our breaths heavy with desire. And you'd think we would jump onto the bed to fuck, but we both take a moment to admire each other. Chase stares at me with the same admiration he does every time he sees me naked.

He leans and kisses me slowly this time, and I melt into him. This man has a way of kissing that tells me without words just how much I mean to him.

With gentle hands, Chase removes my glasses and places them on the nightstand, making everything a little blurry.

"I don't think I'm ever going to get over how fucking perfect you are," he murmurs, his right hand grazing over my side from my ribs to my hip. "I've never felt this way with anyone. It was always just physical in the past, but it's different with you. I see a future with you, which might seem fucking insane for a twenty-year-old to say, but it's true. I don't care that we've only known each other for a short time. When you walked into my life, I instantly felt it. I knew there was something special about you, and I was desperate to get to know you better. Even from day one, it was always more than just physical. Sure, I still wanted to fall into bed with you. I *am* a young guy, after all."

I laugh at his silly joke, but it makes breathing a little easier. The emotion of this moment is almost suffocating, but not in a negative way. I've never had anyone say such sweet words to me, and it's a bit overwhelming. But I don't want him to stop.

"But I wanted something more than sex with you. I think I even would have settled for friendship because there was this voice in the back of my head screaming that I needed you in my life, in whatever capacity that might be. I'm completely thankful you agreed to more than just friendship." Even though his face is fuzzy, I can still tell his smile is filled with love. I know for a fact no one has ever looked at me the way he does.

"You know how nervous I was to take a chance on you," I tell him, taking a step closer and placing my hand on his neck. My fingers play with his hair a little as I try to find the right words. "I put you in a box because you were a jock. I figured that because we came from two different worlds, there could be no way we'd actually work. There was also this fear that you didn't really want me. And even if you did, it would only be for a night or two. I didn't want to risk my heart getting broken. I know now you aren't the kind of guy I feared you would be.

"I also figured out along the way that I had a negative view of sports because of my father. It was never really sports that I hated, it was my dad and the way he viewed sports. It was his fucked-up thinking that I hated, and I twisted that negativity and put it onto all sports and anyone who enjoyed them. But you've taught me I was wrong. You helped me take so many negative memories from my past and replace them with better ones. I probably won't ever be as into sports as you are, but I see the joy that you do now. You've changed me for the better. There isn't any way I can ever truly thank you for that."

"You don't have to thank me," he assures me, resting his forehead on mine.

When we first arrived at his apartment, I knew we would end up naked, but I wasn't planning on baring my soul like this. But it feels right, and Chase's honest words ease the fear inside me. I'm still not positive we are going to be able to make things work after this school year ends, but I want to try. Because what we are building is worth fighting for.

"I want you inside me," I whisper, tilting my chin and smiling when his lips touch mine.

With gentle hands, he guides me to the bed, and I already know that tonight is going to be different. We aren't just going to fuck. We're going to make love, and that's a first for me. Sex is something we can get from anyone, but this connection, this love, is something that doesn't come around often. I vow to cherish this moment. Even if we do end up not working out in the long run, I know, without a shadow of a doubt, that I will never forget tonight.

When the back of my thighs hit the bed, Chase helps me lay down. He follows, hovering over me and kissing me gently. His cock sits heavy on mine, but he isn't grinding into me. He's taking his time, showing me with his body how much he cares for me.

I've always been a firm believer that actions speak louder than words, and Chase is the prime example of how someone should act in a relationship. He uses all the right words, but he does better than that—he shows me every day what I mean to him, whether it's holding my hand in public or sending me DoorDash when I'm holed in my room studying. Or, like right now, he's telling me he loves me, but he's also using his body to prove it to me. He could easily be rushing this so he can get inside me and fuck me until he comes, but he's taking his time. I'm not just an easy fuck to him. I'm his boyfriend—the man he loves—and holy shit, does that feel amazing.

Chase's lips leave mine, but they don't leave my body. They trail kisses along my jawline, down my neck, and across my torso. He pauses at my nipple and laps at it before sucking the bud between his lips, his teeth grazing over the sensitive spot, causing my cock to spasm. I've never had someone pay my nipples much attention in the past, and I'm quickly learning they are a huge turn-on for me.

After my attentive quarterback has thoroughly explored my chest, he continues his path downward. Goose bumps erupt all over my body when he tickles my V with his tongue, then blows on the area.

Chase has always been an unselfish lover, but tonight, he's really pulling out all the stops.

When he finally gets to my throbbing cock, I'm expecting him to swallow me down, and I can't help but jut my hips toward him. To my dismay, he buries his nose in my groin and takes a deep inhale. "Fuck, you smell so good," he notes.

I'm not sure how good I smell after spending a couple of hours in the car, but I'll take his word for it all the same. Who am I to tell him he's wrong? If he gets off on my scent, I'm not going to complain.

Just when I think he's going to blow me, he takes another surprise detour and pushes my legs up. I whimper, but it's in anticipation of what is to come. My cock throbs, feeling the same build-up I am.

Oh shit. Is Chase about to do what I think he's about to do? I had a shower this morning, and I always pay close attention to every inch of my body, so I know I'm clean, but a part of me still wants to protest.

Chase must notice me tense up because he pauses and looks at me. "Are you okay?" he asks.

"I've never had anyone's mouth there before," I confess.

"You're telling me I get to be the first person to eat this gorgeous ass?" he questions, and I nod. "Fuck, that turns me on so much, baby. I promise I'll make you feel so good you'll be begging for me to rim you every night." I nibble on my lower lip but slowly dip my chin. "If you hate it, I'll stop, and if you're entirely against the idea, I won't force you to do this," he assures me.

"I want to try," I tell him. "I'm just nervous I won't taste very good."

"Let me be the judge of that, baby." He runs his cheek up the side of my leg, his stubble tickling me a little. "If you absolutely hate it, tell me, and I'll stop. I promise."

He's always honest with me and has never given me any reason to distrust him, so I give him permission to go ahead.

"I bet you're going to taste amazing," he murmurs, getting himself in position and pushing my legs up a little more.

My knees rest against my chest, and I feel a little like a pretzel, but those thoughts fade instantly when Chase's tongue swirls my pucker, causing red-hot need to course through my veins. My cock throbs with desire as he continues to circle my entrance, and a small bead of precum forms at my slit. His tongue feels so good that it has my toes curling in the air.

A needy mewl escapes me when his tongue slips past my tight rings and enters me. "Fuck!" I cry out, my head falling back while he fucks me with his tongue.

"You taste so fucking good, baby, just like I knew you would," he tells me before diving back in to eat me out.

I'm a panting mess as he devours me. My heart is beating

so hard I can feel it in my head. And the growls coming from my man tell me he's loving this just as much, if not better.

He pauses briefly, reaching a hand up to my face, his fingers dancing over my lips. "Suck them for me, baby. Get them good and wet so I can stretch you for me."

I do as I'm told, sucking his fingers into my mouth, twirling my tongue around them, slurping them like they're his cock. My dick twitches at the thought, and Chase kisses my crown.

"I'd suck your cock if I wasn't afraid that you'd come too soon. I want to make tonight last, so don't you dare come until I tell you," he commands, slipping his fingers out of my mouth as I nod. Then he lowers his head back to my needy pucker.

He kisses my entrance, nipping, causing my back to bow. "I love how responsive your body is to me," he muses out loud before shoving his tongue inside me once again.

I cry out when one finger joins his tongue. My body is so hot and my cock throbs, laying heavy against my stomach, twitching with need as he works me up.

I'm a fucking mess as Chase prepares me, and as much as I'm dying to beg for more, I don't want to rush this either. Tonight is special. I'm going to let my man take as long as he wants. It's only going to make the orgasm that much more intense. At least, that is what I'm telling myself. I don't think I have ever been so worked up.

"Look at you swallowing my fingers," Chase tells me, sliding in a second finger and scissoring them to stretch my hole. "You're so fucking tight. I can only imagine what it's going to feel like when my cock finally gets inside you. I bet you're going to choke it to death."

His dirty words cause tingles to erupt throughout my entire body.

"Do you want me, baby?" he asks, changing the angle of

his fingers to hit my prostate, making it hard to breathe, let alone think straight.

"Jeeesssuuusss," I hiss out between my teeth when he nails it again, pausing to massage it. My cock twitches again, bobbing off my body.

"Do you think you can come untouched?" he questions.

He's fingered my ass a bunch of times but never long enough to test his theory, but now I'm dying to know. However, I want it to be his cock that makes me come.

He slides his hand back briefly to insert a third finger, and I pant heavily. Fuck, I love how full I feel right now, but it's not enough.

"More… I need you," I plead. "I want your cock. Pllleeease give it to me."

"Do you think you're ready?" he inquires, and I nod quickly.

He's a lot bigger than just his three fingers, but I don't care. I don't want to wait a second longer. I need him inside me *now*.

His face is fuzzy, but I think he tilts his head to his night-stand. "Get the lube and a condom," he instructs, and I turn as much as I can with his fingers still inside me to grab the items, fumbling around a little to find the items without perfect vision.

As soon as I hand him the condom, he slides his fingers out of me. I can't help but whimper and pout at the empty feeling.

"Don't worry, baby, I won't leave you wanting long," he assures me while tearing open the condom wrapper and sliding it on his cock.

After the condom is secured, he takes the lube from me and pours a dollop on his fingers, warming it up before circling my hole and shoving two digits inside me, making sure I'm nice and wet for him.

Once he's done lubing me up, he slickens his

cock. "Ready, baby?" he inquires, lining himself up with my entrance.

"Fuck me, handsome," I beg.

"With fucking pleasure," he says, pushing his hips forward.

His tip circles around my pucker a few times, then pushes in. The broad head of his cock impales me, stealing my breath as he slowly works his way past my tight ring.

Chase gasps. "Holy. Fucking. Shit. Balls." His words are strained, and his breathing is as labored as mine. "I knew you'd be tight, but *damn...*" He pauses, taking slow, deep breaths and muttering something under his breath. It kind of sounds like he's listing off legal terms, which almost makes me want to chuckle.

"Sorry," he whispers after a moment. "You feel too good. I'm just trying not to come prematurely."

"Take all the time you need, baby," I assure him. "We've got nowhere we need to be."

He nods, pushing forward more. Inch by inch, my ass swallows him, and I pant with need. He feels even better than I dreamed he would. He's fucking huge, and I know I'm going to feel him tomorrow, but I don't care. Actually, I want to feel him tomorrow. I can't wait to feel the burn after, a constant reminder of this moment.

Once he's fully inside, he bends over to kiss me, allowing us both a moment to adjust.

"I love you," he whispers against my lips.

"I love you too."

I never meant any words more. I love Chase Anderson with my entire being. He bombarded his way into my life like a Golden Retriever puppy desperate for pets and stayed there until I let down my walls.

My heart now belongs to him, and I wouldn't have it any other way.

CHAPTER TWENTY-TWO

NOTHING HAS EVER FELT so earth-shatteringly good as being buried balls deep inside Gabe. When I first entered him, he was so fucking tight I was terrified I was going to blow in two seconds. To prevent it, I had to think of boring legal terms from my class.

Now I'm fully inside his hot channel, kissing him tenderly, and there is nowhere else I'd rather be. No moment has ever been this right. I'd give up the world to be where I am right now—Gabe in my arms and his body flushed that gorgeous shade of pink. Sweat covers us and needy mewls slip past my man's lips as I shallowly thrust into him.

Football has always been number one in my life, with my family a close second, but Gabe is creeping his way up the list. It won't be long before he's my new number one. Hell, he might already be. Any time I think about leaving him, even to play for the NFL, I want to throw up. I didn't think it was possible for anyone to make me feel that way.

When I pictured leaving my family to play for a team far away, it hurt, but it wasn't anything like the soul-deep ache I feel when I think about being away from Gabe.

I don't want to give up football, and Gabe would never allow me to do it for him. So if something happens and I'm drafted by a team other than Michigan, I'll just have to figure out how to keep Gabe in my life. But how do I do that when I don't want him to compromise his life for me?

"I need you to move," Gabe begs, pulling me out of my depressing thoughts. His voice is raspy with need, and his breath is hot against my lips. "Show me what you got, handsome. Use my body. Fuck me like you mean it."

I smile at him, and he gives me a hot, searing kiss before lifting my upper body. I push his knees to his chest, giving myself a fantastic view, pull my hips back until my cock almost falls out of him then I slam forward.

"Yes!" Gabe shouts, so I do it again and again.

His channel has a tight hold on me, milking me as I thrust into him hard and fast. Sweat drips down my back when I pick up my pace, shifting my hips slightly, watching the way his body jolts when I nail his prostate. His cock bobs against his body, the smallest amount of precum leaking from the tip. The sight fills me with pride.

"Are you going to come hands-free for me, baby?" I question, continuing to pound him with everything I've got.

"I-I-I think so," he stammers.

A tingle deep in my spine spreads throughout my body, and my balls draw up as my orgasm nears. "Come for me, baby," I plead, fucking him as hard and fast as I can.

"Fuuucck," he screams, his channel clamping down on me as small spurts of cum erupt from his perfect cock, coating his lower abdomen.

"Yesss," I hiss out and spill my release into the condom. My pace wavers, and I grind into Gabe, needing to be deeper. My legs shake, and my vision darkens a little as I ride through the most intense orgasm of my life. I grab his cock and stroke, needing to milk him dry like his body is doing to me.

My head spins when I thrust one last time, and I collapse forward, barely able to catch myself on my forearms so that I don't crush my man.

"Holy fuck," he whispers.

"My thoughts exactly," I reply, lowering Gabe's legs. He wraps them around me and holds me close.

My cock starts to soften, and I know I need to pull out of him so that the condom doesn't slip off, but I don't want to move. Reluctantly, the smarter side of my brain takes over, and I slide out of him, tying the condom off and tossing it in the trash can beside my bed. Once it's discarded, I lay on my back and bring him into my arms, where he cuddles up, resting his head on my chest.

"I'm sticky," he murmurs after a few minutes, and I chuckle.

"Want to shower together?" I check.

"Yes, but my entire body feels like Jell-O. I'm probably going to need you to support me so I don't fall over," he replies.

"Having you in my arms is never a hardship," I assure him.

Slowly, I sit up and slide out of bed, offering him a hand. He takes it, and I help him stand before pulling him to my bathroom. Gabe leans against me as I turn on the water and wait for it to warm up.

"I don't think I've ever orgasmed so hard in my entire life," he tells me.

"It was crazy-intense, wasn't it? I'll admit, watching you come just from my dick was hot as fuck."

The corners of his lips tip upward, and he buries his face into my chest a little as if trying to hide.

Once the water is hot, I pull him inside and begin to wash him, starting with his hair. My fingers dig in to give him a massage that must be amazing, considering he's damn near purring.

"You've got magic hands," he mutters, and I chuckle.

"You've told me that before," I tease, and he bats lazily at my chest.

I help him rinse, then rub his shoulders before moving to his pecs, then down to his stomach, washing away the dried cum.

Gabe isn't very hairy, unlike me—another difference between us. I have to manscape like crazy to avoid looking like a gorilla. Don't get me wrong, there are lots of guys who love that, but for some reason, I just don't like that much hair on my body. So, I keep my hair as short as possible. I considered waxing once, but I don't want to be completely hair free, just more under control.

After his stomach is clean, I kneel before him, washing his balls and dick, making sure not to linger for long. Both of us are exhausted from the amazing sex we just had and should have a nap before round two. I move onto his legs, then turn him around to clean his sensitive hole, washing away as much of the lube as I can.

Slowly, I rise back to my feet, wash his back, and rinse him off. By the time I'm done, his eyelids are drooping, and a giant yawn slips past his lips.

"Why don't you go dry off and lay down," I suggest. "I'll join you in a couple of minutes."

"You don't want me to return the favor?" he asks, yawning again.

I smile at him and shake my head. "Next time, but you're exhausted. I promise I won't be long."

He doesn't say anything right away, and I wonder if he's going to argue, but when he yawns for a third time, I give him a gentle shove out of the shower. "Go rest," I insist.

Finally, he listens, grabbing a towel before slipping out of the bathroom.

I don't take my time when it comes to washing my own body, wanting to be in bed and holding my man. As soon as I'm done, I shut off the water and step out, grabbing a towel and rushing to the bedroom, where Gabe is almost asleep.

"Took you long enough," he teases with a sleepy voice.

"Sorry, I tried to hurry."

He chuckles and waves me off. "I'm just joking. Now come here and hold me," he says, holding the blanket up for me to crawl in.

Once I'm under the blankets with him, I wrap him in my arms, and he rests his head on my chest, playing with my neatly trimmed chest hair.

It doesn't take long before his breathing evens out, and I'm certain he's asleep. I love falling asleep with Gabe in my arms and wonder if I could convince him to sleep here every night. It doesn't make sense for him to move in when I'll be moving out at the end of this upcoming semester, and he still has one year left of law school. But I don't want to be away from him more than I have to.

Who knew I would find someone who makes me love them more than football?

CHAPTER TWENTY-THREE

NANA PLACES the cheesecake she made for Chase in the refrigerator, then tilts her head toward the kitchen table. "Sit," she commands, and I do as I'm told.

I might be an adult, but I wouldn't put it past her to slap me upside the head in a loving kind of way for not listening.

"Tell me more about this boy you love," she says, sitting in the chair across from mine.

I've been so busy with school and Chase that Nana and I haven't really had a chance to sit down and talk that much. We still have our morning phone calls, but those are always rushed and never feel like the right time to spill my guts. And Nana isn't a pusher. She lets me come to her when I'm ready.

"I never told you I love him," I murmur.

She laughs, shaking her head. "Oh, sweet summer child, you think I don't see the way your face lights up when you talk about him. Or how this is the first time you're bringing someone home to meet me. Stop playing stupid and just admit you love him."

I chuckle and sigh. "I do love him, Nana. He's amazing. He treats me like gold and has even got me enjoying football."

"Are you sure you're not dating a wizard?" she questions with a joyful grin. "I feel like it would take real magic to turn someone like you into a sports fan of any kind."

I laugh along with her. "I thought the same thing. He's helping heal me, taking away the bad memories and replacing them with good ones. Just like you did when I was younger."

"He sounds perfect for you," she notes.

"He is. But he also scares me. He's an amazing quarterback, and there is a strong possibility he'll be drafted in April. What am I going to do if he has to move across the country? What if he forgets about me?" I tell her, voicing all my concerns for the first time.

"If he loves you half as much as you love him, that won't be possible," she tells me.

I worry my bottom lip but nod. I know I have to put my faith in us, that our love is strong enough to keep us together, but we're both young, and he'll have so many new and shiny things thrown at him when he joins the NFL.

What if I'm no longer good enough for him?

"Stop worrying about the what-ifs," Nana states, reading me like a book. She's always been good at that. "Love is powerful, don't doubt it. If I feel like that boy doesn't love you the way he should, I'll let you know."

I chuckle, and the doorbell rings. "I guess you'll find out soon enough," I say and rush to let Chase in.

"Hello, gorgeous," he greets, dipping his chin to kiss me. I think it was meant to be chaste, but it quickly deepens, eliciting lust-filled tingles to explode throughout my body.

"Well, that's one way to greet someone," Nana voices, humor in her tone.

I groan and bury my head into Chase's chest before taking a deep breath and stepping back. "Chase, this is my nana, Annett. Nana, this is Chase, my boyfriend."

"It's nice to meet you, ma'am," Chase says, taking a step toward my nana and reaching out his hand.

She eyes it for a moment but doesn't return his handshake.

"You can call me Netty or Nana, and I'm more of a hugger if that is okay with you."

Chase smiles and nods. "My mom is the same way," he replies before pulling my petite grandmother into his arms, making her look even smaller.

"Oh, he's a good hugger!" Nana notes.

I nod. "His whole family gives good hugs."

"But mine are the best, right?" he checks.

"Of course," I assure him with a tip of my chin.

"We were going to order Chinese food for supper," Nana tells Chase. "It's a weird New Year's Eve tradition we started when Gabriel started college. Is that okay with you? Gabriel mentioned you're on some kind of diet, so I'm willing to stray from tradition if you need us to."

"Chinese is fine," he assures her. "I just can't indulge too much, but a little bit won't hurt."

"I'll make sure to order a variety of things and avoid too many deep-fried dishes," she says, then walks away to call in the order.

"She's sweet," Chase tells me once she leaves the room.

"She's the best. Without her, I wouldn't have made it the first couple of years of college."

"She means a lot to you, doesn't she?" he inquires.

"She was my world before I met you," I whisper.

When I look into his eyes, desire is evident but so is love. "Do you have any idea what it means to me when you say things like that?" he asks, and I shake my head. "It drives me crazy. Sometimes I don't think it's possible that you could love me as much I do you, but then you say shit like that, and I believe it."

"I love you so much it's scary. You hold my heart in your hands," I whisper.

"I'll protect it like the treasure it is," he vows.

"Who's ready to watch some cars get blown up?" Nana questions when she gets back to the room.

Chase quirks a brow at me, and I chuckle. "Another tradition. We watch action movies. One year, we decided to try something new and spent the evening playing *Just Dance*. Nana could barely walk for a week after, so we decided it was safer to stick to movies."

"We could change the genre up if you have something against action movies, though," Nana offers. "Although I'm not sure I want my grandson dating someone with subpar taste."

Chase throws his head back, laughing. "Your nana is amazing," he tells me before turning his attention back to her. "I love action movies, so there's no need to stray from tradition on my behalf."

She nods. "Good. You can stay for now, then." With those words, she heads to the living room, and we follow behind, snickering.

The Chinese food shows up about thirty minutes into the first movie, making Chase whine a little. "We were just getting to the good part."

"Nana lets us eat in the living room on New Year's Eve," I inform him, making his face light up.

"That's awesome."

"I am pretty fantastic if I do say so myself," Nana says with a toothy grin as she stands to pay the delivery man, but Chase stops her.

"Please, let me pay for it," he pleads, but Nana shoots him a look that makes him freeze.

"It's your birthday! If for even one second you think I'm going to allow you to pay, you've got another thing coming. Now make yourself useful and grab the bags," she commands. "Gabriel, you get the plates out of the cupboard."

"Yes, ma'am," I reply, rushing to the kitchen.

Chase isn't far behind me, placing the containers on the counter so we can dish up.

"Your nana can be kind of scary," he whispers, and I chuckle.

"Yeah, it's best to just listen to her because she has no problem putting you in your place. It doesn't matter that you are more than double her size."

"The small ones are always the scariest," he murmurs.

"Are you calling me scary?" I tease.

"I haven't seen that side of you yet, but I'm sure you can be," he insists as he dishes up his food, avoiding the deep-fried dishes. "Only one more game to go, then I can let go a little more."

"I admire the dedication you have for your sport," I tell him with an easy grin.

"Football was my life until I met you," he says, and his words hit me in the gut, and the air wooshes out of me. I wasn't expecting him to say something like that. It feels like a stronger statement than the one I made.

"I love you, gorgeous," he whispers, leaning in for another kiss.

"Hurry up and dish up, boys. I need to know what happens next," Nana states when she enters the kitchen.

"We've seen this movie at least ten times," I remind her.

She rolls her eyes, waving her hand around. "Pish posh, at my age, you forget everything. That means you can watch movies like it's the first time over and over again."

I sigh. "You're not senile, Nana."

She doesn't bother arguing further, grabs a plate, and dishes up.

We end up watching three movies by the time midnight approaches, and we do the countdown, staring at Nana's grandfather clock. "Five… four… three… two… one… *Happy New Year,*" we all shout at the same time.

Chase pulls me into his arms to plant a kiss on my lips, then leans over and kisses Nana's cheek, making her blush.

"It seems blushing runs in your family," Chase notes.

"I'm glad my grandson has someone like you in his life," Nana tells him. "You make him glow with joy. Thank you for loving him."

I blink back tears at Nana's words. I'm not normally a guy who cries. Maybe it's the fact I'm beyond exhausted. *Yeah… we'll go with that.* Chase has been keeping me up late every night, so I'm highly emotional.

"I'm the lucky one to have him in my life," Chase tells Nana, making more tears bubble to the surface.

I take a deep breath and blink a few more times before I find my voice. "If everyone is done being sappy, Chase and I are going to go," I declare.

"I packed you a piece of cheesecake to go," Nana tells Chase, who beams at her.

"You're the best," he says, hugging her. "Are you sure you don't want to come to my championship game on Sunday?"

We discussed his game between shows and eating cake. I know she would say yes if the game were here, but having to fly isn't appealing to her.

"I'm sorry, but I promise I'll get over my fear of flying when you make it to the Super Bowl," she assures him.

"I'm going to hold you to that," he says, taking my hand and waiting for the piece of cheesecake she rushes to grab.

"Tonight was fucking amazing," Chase tells me as we walk to his car. "Thank you for making this the best birthday ever."

In response, I lean in for a kiss. "How 'bout you take me back to your place so I can give you your present," I flirt, batting my eyes.

His brows shoot up, and he races to his car, dragging me along. "Best birthday ever!" His shout fills the night air, followed by my laughter.

Tonight really was fucking perfect, but every day with Chase is.

CHAPTER TWENTY-FOUR

ONE WEEK LATER

SWEAT TRICKLES down my back as I stare down the field. We're ahead by two points, and there isn't much time left on the clock, but we can't let our guard down even for a second. I can taste the fucking win, but everyone knows it only takes one wrong move, and everything can change.

I refuse to let that happen.

The crowd is almost half filled with people cheering for us and half against us. Which isn't how it normally is, but it's the championship game, and the fans for both sides are out to support their chosen teams.

I check on either side of me, making sure my teammates are in position and ready, then yell, "Hike," and our center snaps the ball into my hands.

I drop back and scan the field. My first option is Mikey, but he's blocked. So my eyes flash to my second option, who is also covered. No one is available, and the pocket is collapsing, so I have to scramble. I run as hard and fast as I can, dodging the opposing team to the best of my ability. My focus is on the goal line and the best path to get there. I try to avoid thinking about the ticking of the clock, but it's there in the back of my mind.

So many times, I narrowly miss a body lunging at me,

making me so thankful I've worked extra hard on my agility this year. When I finally cross into the end zone and throw the ball down, scoring our team a touchdown, the crowd's roar is deafening. My heart is racing so hard that I feel like I might pass out.

My teammates join me, shouting as loudly as they can. We just won the fucking championship.

The GSU Koalas are fucking championship winners.

A bunch of guys lift me onto their shoulders in celebration, and I laugh so hard my lungs hurt. When they finally set me on my feet, I take a moment to scan the crowd rushing the field, looking for my family, Gabe, and Rio.

When my eyes finally land on them, I push my way through the crowd, pulling Gabe into my arms and smashing my lips to his.

"You did so good," he tells me when I pull back.

"I feel like I'm high right now," I admit before turning to hug my family.

"I'm proud of you, son," Dad tells me, clapping me on the shoulder.

"At least one of us could be a championship winner," Rio says with a warm smile. He might be sad about his loss, but he's still happy for me.

We chat until the families are escorted out of the way and the team is lined up for the trophy ceremony. A giant smile is permanently on my face the entire time. I had my heart set on this win, but it feels almost surreal that it actually happened.

The ceremony goes by in a blur, and before I know it, I'm in an eighteen-plus bar surrounded by my teammates, celebrating our win. Everyone over twenty-one has bright pink wristbands on, letting the bartenders know we can drink.

Gabe is by my side the entire time, laughing and having a good time with my friends. I couldn't ask for anything more than this right now, well, except maybe to be naked and alone with my man, but that can wait for our own private after-party.

"You're going to have all the teams wanting you in April," Mikey says, slurring his words a little. "If you aren't drafted in the first round, I'm going to be so fucking shocked I'll probably die."

I laugh at him and clap him on the shoulder. "Thanks, man. I'm praying I'll end up with Michigan, but we'll see what fate has in store for me. My agent keeps assuring me that they want me, but you know how the draft works, and they don't have first pick this year, so it's anyone's guess as to who I'll end up with."

He nods a hell of a lot like he's lost in his own head. "Fate does what fate does," he murmurs before wandering off to talk to someone else. *Man, he's drunk.*

"You're not drinking," I say to Gabe with a lifted brow.

"I'd rather not be drunk in a city I don't know. Obviously, you'd have my back, but I don't want to chance it anyway. You have as much as you want, though. You are twenty-one, after all, and haven't even had a chance to get drunk in a bar yet."

I shrug. "I'm good with just one beer. Besides, I'm thinking we should make up an excuse to leave soon."

"Oh? Do you have something else you want to do instead?" he asks, leaning in and waggling his brows.

"Yeah, you," I reply, quickly kissing him before saying goodbye to the guys around me and finding Rio to let him know I'm heading out.

"You're leaving, aren't you?" Rio asks when I find him, and I nod.

"Do you want to leave with us?" I question, but he shakes his head.

"I'm good. I'll see you in the morning," he tells me.

With Gabe's hand in mine, we walk out of the bar and down the street to our hotel. GSU provided all the players with hotel rooms, but we had to share, and that wasn't going to work for me. Besides, Gabe also needed a place to stay, so my parents booked an extra room when booking theirs. Thankfully, our room is on a separate floor from my parents because I would hate for Gabe to turn me down tonight. I want to celebrate my win in our bed, doing the horizontal boogie or whatever that saying is.

The hotel is only a short walk away, and as soon as we are in our room, I have Gabe pressed against the door, my lips sealing his in a grueling kiss.

"I can't believe I'm about to have sex with a champion," Gabe teases, making me chuckle. "I'm one lucky guy."

I nip at his lips. "I'm the lucky one, baby. I wouldn't have been able to play if it wasn't for your tutoring."

"Well, since we're both clearly to thank here, we should definitely celebrate, but we're wearing too many clothes," he states, moving to undo the button on my jeans.

We strip out of our clothes at a rapid speed, and the second we're naked, Gabe pulls me into him. I'm already leaking as usual, and he swipes the palm of his hand over the head of my throbbing cock, using my precum as lube so he can jack me off.

"Watching you play your heart out today really turned me on," he whispers in a breathy tone, moving his fist up and down. "Since you're the real winner, I want you to choose how we fuck tonight."

"I want you to ride me," I tell him, walking backward. His hand stays on me the entire way, and once the back of my thighs hits the bed, I climb on and lay down.

Gabe lets me go at that moment and rushes to his suitcase for what I'm assuming are supplies.

"You won't have to stretch me," he tells me when he gets back. I quirk a brow at him, confused as fuck at his statement. "When we got changed after dinner, I prepared a surprise for you." He turns around and bends over, showing me the plug in his ass.

"Fuck, that's hot," I breathe out.

"Take it out so I can ride you," he requests, and there's no way I'm arguing with him.

He climbs on the bed, giving me better access, and sheaths my cock as I slip the plug out of him. Then he turns around and straddles me, reaching behind him to grab my cock. He lines me up with his entrance, slowly sliding down, a needy mewl slipping past his lips when he takes me inside him.

"Fuck, you look so hot on top of me like that," I tell him.

He licks his lips. "You… feel… so good… inside me," he replies through panted breaths.

I groan as he continues his descent. "Take it all, baby."

Fully seated on me, he leans down to nibble at my lips and steals my breath away with a toe-curling kiss. *Can he feel the way my dick is twitching inside him?*

"Ride me, gorgeous," I encourage him after a few amazing kisses. "Use me to get off. Show me what you got."

He listens eagerly, shifting his hips in circular motions, not moving up and down just yet, but fuck, does it feel amazing.

Our breaths are labored, and heavy pants fill the space of our room. A thin layer of sweat covers our bodies, and when Gabe places his hand on my chest for balance, I'm certain he can feel the way my heart is racing.

"Give it to me, baby," I plead, needing more.

This time he really starts to ride me, bouncing up and down on my throbbing cock.

"Fuck," I groan as he picks up his pace. "You're so fucking sexy."

He smirks at me, but his mouth falls open, and he cries out when I raise a hand to pinch his nipple. "Yes!"

I buck my hips, fucking him from the bottom, causing needy mewls and whimpers to leave my man's lips.

When he slams down on me again, my toes curl, and a jolt of electricity shoots through my body, telling me I'm not going to last. I grab Gabe's bobbing erection, stroking him in rhythm with his movements. Even though I know he can come hands-free, I don't have the patience to wait for it tonight. My orgasm is so fucking close I can taste it, and I want him to come with me.

"So close," he moans out. I use my free hand to pinch his nipple again, this time harder. "Fuck, fuck, *fuck!*" he shouts as his climax takes over, shooting his load over my chest and stomach, a drop hitting my chin, which would make me grin if his channel wasn't clamped down on me so tight, making it hard to breathe.

Moving my hands to his hips, I buck into him as hard as I can, chasing my release. It doesn't take long for my balls to draw up and for me to fall over the edge, coming so hard my eyes roll into the back of my head.

Gabe collapses on top of me, not caring that he's lying in his cum. I hold him as our heart rates lower and our breathing returns to normal, but eventually, I have to let him go so I can dispose of the condom.

"Care to join me for a shower?" I ask once I'm out of bed.

His eyelids are already drooping, and it's obvious it has also been a long day for him. He also always gets sleepy after an orgasm, where I usually get a shot of adrenaline.

"I guess I have to," he murmurs. "I'm covered in cum. I shouldn't have laid on you."

I chuckle. "Why don't I just grab a cloth and clean you up," I offer.

He gives me a sleepy smile. "That would be amazing."

I head to the bathroom, discard the condom, and then warm up a cloth so I can take care of my man. When I return, Gabe's eyes are already shut, but I don't think he's asleep yet.

"That feels nice," he whispers while I clean him up, making sure to wipe away as much cum as possible. I also give a few swipes to his sensitive hole to wipe away the lube.

"Rest well, baby. I'll be back in a little bit," I tell him when I'm finished and kiss his forehead.

While I'm in the shower, I can't help but think how fucking amazing my life is right now. I have a man who's so fucking fantastic, better than anyone I could have ever dreamed up, and a promising career ahead of me in the NFL.

Now, I just have to keep my fingers crossed that I land the team I want when I get drafted.

CHAPTER TWENTY-FIVE

Gabriel

ROUGHLY SEVEN WEEKS LATER

THE PAST TWO months have been like a dream. Chase and I have spent more time together now that he's done playing football for the season. And even though I still have a busy schedule, Chase makes sure to work around it to the best of his ability, never letting a day go by without seeing each other.

He's told me he is addicted to my lips and needs a hit at least once a day. I acted like he was crazy, but it only made me turn to goo on the inside.

Today, he left with his agent to go to Indiana for the NFL Scouting Combine. I'm already missing him, which is obviously ridiculous, but I can't help it. Unfortunately, it also makes me anxious. If I'm already feeling like this, and he's only going to be gone for a couple of days, how am I going to cope if he gets drafted by a team that isn't Michigan?

According to the stats, Chase is ranked in the top ten for the draft, and we are aware multiple teams want him. His agent has made that much clear. He's assured Chase that whoever he ends up with, his contract will be amazing. But Chase doesn't care about the money, not as much as he cares about staying close to his family and me. In the end, the choice isn't his.

"Your face looks weird," Sasha declares when he comes into the living room where I'm studying.

"What is that supposed to mean?" I question.

"It's not weird, it's just sad," Max supplies, and I roll my eyes.

Sasha snaps his fingers. "That's it," he exclaims. "I've gotten used to the goofy smile you've been sporting since Chase walked into your life."

I sigh. "I'm fine."

"You don't look fine," Max counters, and I glare at him.

It's one thing for Sasha to be sassy and make fun of me, but I wasn't expecting Max to join in. Maybe this is his way of paying me back for being too worried about him after his allergic reaction.

"I miss my boyfriend," I hiss out, feeling exasperated. "Is that such a big deal?"

"I think there's more going on than just missing him," Victor adds.

Great, now everyone is in on this. Pushing my glasses up, I pinch the bridge of my nose and try to figure out how to get my friends off my back. I don't want to talk about this because I know if I do, I'm going to become emotional, and I don't want to show them that side of me right now. But it's hard not to be upset when considering the possibility of losing the best thing that has ever happened to me.

"You know you don't have to break up if he gets drafted by a team other than Michigan, right?" Max checks.

Fuck, I hate how well my friends know me. I guess we're having this conversation whether I like it or not.

"I know we don't have to break up," I reply quietly. "But what's going to keep us together? Love is powerful, but it's not invincible. Distance is hard. On top of that, throw in the challenge of playing for the NFL, and the difficulty level goes up by a hundred. Chase's entire focus is going to have to be on the game and proving to his team they made the right choice. He can't be distracted by me." My voice wavers at those words, and I think back to my conversation with his agent last night.

"Chase has so much potential," Alexander tells me after Chase excuses himself to the bedroom to take a call.

I smile and nod. "He's so talented. I've never seen anyone move like he does."

"The first few years in the NFL are the hardest," he informs me. "All eyes are going to be on Chase to see if he's going to remain on his A-game. Distractions aren't something he can risk having in his life."

I tip my chin in agreement, but his words make me uneasy.

"I know the two of you are in love, but if you want Chase to be at his best, maybe you should consider letting him go. Obviously, he'll be upset, but I'm positive you can convince him it's for his own good. We all want Chase to succeed, and sometimes sacrifices have to happen."

His words cut deep into my soul, making it hard to breathe. How the hell am I supposed to respond? Before I have the chance to form a sentence, Chase is back with a big grin.

"Sorry about that," he apologizes. "It was one of my sponsors wanting to wish me good luck at the Combine."

The smile I flash him is tight, but I'm trying not to let him know how affected I am by Alexander's words. The truth is, I've been worried for a while about exactly what Alexander brought up.

Now, I feel selfish for not wanting to let Chase go.

"You're not a distraction," Victor states in a firm tone, bringing me back to the present. "You're his boyfriend, not some fling. Yes, it's going to be challenging, but if you both put your all into it, you can get through it. Besides, it will only be a year, then you can join him. You can practice law anywhere. With how smart you are, law firms all over the country are going to want you working for them."

I take a shaky breath but shrug. "What if the distance is too hard on Chase, and he starts making mistakes? I can't be the reason he fails."

Sasha wraps his arms around me, pulling me in for a hug. "Oh, sweetie," he coos, and I can't keep back the tears any longer. "Have you told him this is how you feel?"

I shake my head against his neck.

"This is a conversation the two of you must have," Max voices.

"He's just going to say something sweet and tell me not to worry," I reply. "His agent told me I should break up with him."

"Ex-fucking-cuse me?" Sasha blurts out.

"He said exactly what I've been afraid of. He told me sometimes sacrifices have to be made."

Sasha growls, and I can feel the vibrations through his chest. "Oh, I'm going to fucking murder this guy."

"You need to tell Chase about this," Victor tells me. "That's all kinds of fucked up. I know the guy is only worried about the money he makes off Chase and *not* what is best for him. You are what's best for him! I sure as hell wouldn't want someone like that representing me. I bet Chase won't either."

"Since you can't talk to Chase until he gets back, maybe you should talk to Rio. He knows Chase better than we do. He's also a college athlete, so maybe he'll have better advice," Max advises.

"That isn't a bad idea. I love Chase too much to hurt him in any way, but football has always been his everything. I can't be the reason he fails at that."

My friends sit with me until I'm not afraid I will fall apart anymore. Eventually, I work up the courage to text Rio, and he invites me over.

I hope my friends are right, and talking with someone closer to Chase will give me more clarity.

"How's it going?" Rio asks when he lets me in.

"Been better," I murmur.

"Missing the big guy already?" he teases.

"Yeah, but I'm also worried."

"What about?" he questions as we head to the couches.

"Alexander, Chase's agent, told me to break up with him. He thinks I'm going to be too much of a distraction and affect Chase's game. There is already going to be so much pressure on his shoulders. I don't want to be the one who kills his dreams."

"Are you fucking kidding me?" Rio shouts, startling me and causing me to jump a little. "Who the fuck does that guy think he is?" I've never seen him angry before, but he looks like he's ready to murder Chase's agent. "You have to tell Chase about that the second he gets back. I've always thought that guy was a weasel, but I never had any proof until now. He doesn't care about Chase and his career or his life. He only cares about the money."

"But don't you think he's right on some level? I *am* going to be a distraction," I whisper.

Rio shakes his head. "You're the opposite of a distraction to Chase. You're his new finishing line. You're the reason he gets up in the morning. He's going to play his ass off in the NFL *because* of you. To make you proud. You make him a better player. He was high-ranked before the two of you started dating, but his ranking went up after. Each game you came to had him playing harder than he ever has. So, Alexander can get fucked with his backward way of thinking."

I gasp, suddenly finding it hard to breathe. I wouldn't have believed the words had they come from Chase, but Rio is a third party who doesn't have as much invested in this as we do. He wouldn't be saying these things if they weren't true. He loves Chase as a brother and wants what's best for him, just like I do. If he thought for even half a second that I truly was going to hurt Chase's game, he would be siding with Alexander, but he's not, so that has to mean something.

Rio grabs his phone off the coffee table and begins typing away harshly.

"Please tell me you're not texting Chase right now," I beg. "This really *would* be a distraction, and he doesn't need that."

"I'm not texting Chase," he assures me. "I'm texting my agent."

I don't have time to ask why when his phone starts ringing.

"Hey, Cam, are you still taking on athletes?" Rio questions and goes silent while his agent responds. "Excellent. I'm not sure what my buddy's contract looks like with his current agent, but this guy is a weasel. He needs somebody better. Do you think you could meet with him next week and help him out?" Again, he goes silent, and I wiggle in my seat awkwardly. "You're the fucking best, man. I'll talk to you soon." Rio ends the call, smiling at me. "You're almost a lawyer. Do you think you can find a way out of Chase's contract for him?"

I can't help but let out a dry laugh. "I can try," I respond, a small bloom of hope forming in my chest.

I came over here thinking Rio would probably agree with Alexander, and I would have to break up with Chase. Now I feel like maybe I do have a future with the man I love.

We just have to get him away from the weasel.

CHAPTER TWENTY-SIX

THE COMBINE WAS AMAZING. I met so many cool people. It's got me even more excited for the draft which is coming up faster than I thought it would. But even though I had a great time, I'm still excited to be on my way home to my man.

Rio sent me a text saying he and Gabe have a surprise planned for when I'm back, so I head straight to my apartment the instant I land after I say goodbye to Alexander, who's been acting a little weird on our trip.

"Please tell me there is chocolate cheesecake," I call out when I open the front door.

"Obviously, we aren't monsters," Rio states and gives me a bro hug. "How did the Combine go?"

"It was fucking amazing but step out of my way. I need to give my boyfriend an I-missed-you kiss," I tell my friend, who laughs at me.

"You missed me?" Gabe questions. "That's so sad because I didn't even notice you were gone."

I growl at him, pulling him into my arms in a swift motion. His eyes widen a little when his chest hits mine, his pouty lips parting slightly. "Don't lie to me, baby. I know you too well by now. You missed me. Just admit it."

"I will do no such thing," he teases, lifting his chin in defiance.

I chuckle, then smash my lips to his. The second I do, he melts into me, his fingers digging into my back, pulling me as close as possible. He's clinging to me like a baby koala, and I refuse to let him go until we're both ready.

"Okay, that's enough, you two. We've got things we need to discuss," Rio says after a moment.

"And chocolate cheesecake," I add, making Gabe snicker.

"You are an easy man to please," my boyfriend states.

"What can I say? I'm a simple man. Give me my boyfriend, football, and chocolate cake. I couldn't ask for more."

"You forgot your family," he adds.

"Oh yeah, them too."

He shakes his head with a goofy grin. "You're ridiculous, but I love you."

"I love you too. Now let's eat cake."

We dish up our plates and then head for the living room. While we eat, I fill them in on what happened at the Combine. They nod with interest, but Gabe's shoulders are stiff, which seems odd, but I push it aside for now.

"How did you guys manage without my awesome presence?" I ask once I've set my plate on the coffee table.

"It was okay," Gabe murmurs. "But there's something I need to tell you."

"Anything," I assure him.

He closes his eyes, taking a deep breath, but it causes my heart rate to spike. *What the fuck is he going to say?* Please, God, tell me he isn't going to break up with me.

"When you took that call the night before you left, Alexander told me to break up with you. He said I was only going to be a distraction to your game, and I believed him," Gabe tells me, his breath hitching.

I see red. Why the fuck would Alexander say something like that? All I've been doing is saying how madly in love I am with Gabe, and my agent goes and pulls a stunt like this.

He's supposed to have my best interests at heart. If he thinks for one fucking minute that Gabe breaking up with me is a good thing, then he's got this all wrong. It would be the worst thing that ever happened to me. I don't want to live a life without the man who owns my heart.

"You are not a distraction to me, baby," I finally tell Gabe when I feel like I can talk again without exploding.

"I know that now. Rio helped me see things clearer. I'm sorry I let my insecurities get the best of me."

I pull him into my arms, holding him for a moment. "If you ever feel like that again, please come to me. I'll spend every day reminding you what you mean to me if I have to. And even *then*, you wouldn't be a distraction. I can love you and be the best football player possible at the same time, even if I'm drafted by a team on the other side of the country."

All of us are silent for a while. I hate that Alexander would say something so fucked up like this. I don't want a prick like that representing me anymore, but what the hell am I supposed to do? I have a contract with him, and those are usually hard to get out of.

"How am I supposed to work with Alexander now?" I voice my concern.

"You don't," Rio states like it's that simple.

"You know it isn't that easy," I remind him, sounding like a grumpy asshole.

"Alexander owns his own company, right?" Gabe inquires.

"Yeah, he didn't want to answer to anyone, so he was a lone agent for a while. I was actually one of the first athletes he started working for. Now he has a few people who work under him to help with new athletes."

"Can I have a copy of your contract?" he requests. "I'm praying I can find a loophole, and you can get out from under him. I'm obviously not a lawyer yet, but I know a few who will help us once I find something we can stand on."

I kiss the top of his head, hugging him tighter. "I fucking love you," I whisper. "But then I still have to find a new agent, and it's so fucking close to the draft. I'm not even sure that's going to be possible."

"I've got that covered for you, brother," Rio pipes up. "My agent will be here tomorrow to talk to you. He's an amazing guy and is more than eager to take you on if we can get you out of your current contract."

Man, I've got the best people in my life. "Thank you," I tell him, then kiss Gabe's head again. "Both of you."

Gabe pulls away, giving me a quick peck on the lips. "We are here for you. Now go grab that contract so I can start going through it. If he signed you early on, he might not have had the best lawyers to draw up an iron-clad contract. I'm keeping my fingers crossed that there are a few ways we can get you out of this."

The look of determination in his eyes has me believing there is still hope, so I rush to my bedroom to grab my laptop, where a copy of my contract is saved in a special folder.

Gabe takes the laptop from me and starts to read every single word.

"This looks like it's going to take a while. Anyone want another piece of cake?" I ask, making my best friend and Gabe laugh.

Time feels like it's dragging on as Gabe reads my contract. I'm lying on the couch, my feet in Gabe's lap, staring at the ceiling, counting each dot of the popcorn coating. Heaven only knows how long has passed when Gabe finally shouts, "Yes!"

"Did you find something?" I ask, sitting up, careful not to knock the laptop over.

He nods, staring at my computer. "A clause was added stating that the agent will only discuss matters with outside parties with the athlete's approval. Did he ask for your permission to talk to me?"

I shake my head. "Hell, fucking no, he didn't."

Gabe smirks. "I didn't think so. He might be able to push back, claiming that talking to me isn't the same as talking to a professional, but this gives us a leg up. I'm going to send this to my professor, who has already agreed to help us out if I find something. His son is also a lawyer and has offered to represent us if needed."

"Tell him I'm willing to pay him too. I need out of this contract."

He nods and sends off a text. It's late, so I assume the guy won't respond right away. But I'm pleasantly surprised when Gabe's phone rings only a moment later.

"Sorry to bother you so late, Professor O'Callahan," Gabe says when he answers the call, then explains what he found. Then, he sends my contract to his professor and son and sets up a meeting for tomorrow afternoon.

"Professor O'Callahan thinks we can easily get you out of this contract," he tells me after he hangs up.

"Thank fuck," I breathe out, pulling my boyfriend into my arms. "I'm so lucky to have you in my life."

"You are the lucky one," he teases, and I nip at his neck for being sassy. "Professor O'Callahan requested that we send in your bank records when we meet with him and his son tomorrow. Especially for everything you've sent to Alexander."

"I can supply those, no problem. Does he think Alexander was taking too much out?" I ask, and Gabe shrugs.

"There is a possibility. We just want to have all our boxes checked. It will be easier to shut him down if he's done something fraudulent."

I hate to think Alexander would rip me off, but now I'm praying he did. The draft is at the end of next month. I don't have time to let this go through the courts.

Thankfully, I have a super smart boyfriend on my side and some amazing friends.

CHAPTER TWENTY-SEVEN

"ACCORDING TO YOUR CONTRACT, Alexander's fee is two thousand dollars a month plus twenty percent of all sponsorship deals," Cam, Professor O'Callahan's son, says while reading the papers.

"That's right," Chase replies.

"Then how come he's taken out over triple that over the last year?" he questions, glaring at the bank records.

Chase and I both gasp. "What?"

"It started out small," he points out, highlighting January's withdrawal. "And got larger as the year went on, fluctuating here or there, I think, to make it look legit. Did you obtain random new sponsorships in those months?"

Chase shakes his head. "Not that I know of, and if I did, I didn't see a penny of it."

My heart races as I learn with Chase that Alexander was stealing from him. I knew the man was a slimy snake, but I didn't think he was going to be this much of a piece of shit. Seriously, who fucking does this to people?

"That's what I thought," Cam mutters. "I'm going to send Alexander an email asking him to meet with us as soon as possible. I'll make sure to put in lots of scary jargon so he doesn't delay. Hopefully, we'll be able to settle this in a timely manner. Do you want him to pay, or do you just want out of the contract?"

"I just want out. Fuck the money," Chase says, and I reach for his hand, giving it a comforting squeeze. He offers me a small smile in return.

I can't believe this happened to him. But at least this will give him an easier way to get out of the contract.

"That will hopefully be quicker. Unfortunately, it will mean he can continue to rip others off."

Chase growls, his anger clearly bubbling just under the surface, making my heart ache for him even more. "I fucking hate that, but I don't have the time to let this go through the courts. The draft is around the corner. I need a new agent now."

"I understand. Hopefully, someone else will catch on and file their own lawsuit. I'm going to advise you not to talk to anyone else about this. There is a strong possibility Alexander's lawyer is going to serve you with a gag order in order for you to walk away from this contract. He knows how important it is to get out of this contract as fast as possible, and he's not going to let you go easily."

Chase sighs but nods. Fuck, I feel so bad for him. Hopefully, this will all be behind us soon.

"I'll be in touch as soon as I know more," Cam assures us.

"Thank you for your help, and you, too, Professor O'Callahan. We couldn't have done this without your help," I tell them.

"Don't thank us now. We haven't won yet," Professor O'Callahan states, but the smile on his lips tells me he's pretty sure this will be settled soon.

Chase and I leave the lawyer's office hand in hand, and as soon as we get to his car, I pull him into my arms, offering him some comfort after everything he just found out. He holds me for a while, and I refuse to let go until he's ready. Neither of us says anything, just silently embracing in a parking lot.

"Thank you," he whispers when he steps back.

"I'm always here for you," I remind him before we get into his car and head straight for his apartment, where Rio's agent is waiting for us.

"I hope this new guy isn't a dickwad, too," Chase grumbles as he drives.

"Rio trusts him," I remind him.

"I know, and that puts my mind at ease a little, but I trusted Alexander too." He slams his hand on the steering wheel, his anger finally bubbling through. "How could I be so fucking stupid?"

I shake my head and put my hand on his thigh. "You're not stupid. Alexander took advantage of you. He's an asshole, but that doesn't make you dumb. Shit like this happens to people all the time. Please don't beat yourself up over this."

He doesn't respond right away, but he puts his hand on top of mine and squeezes. "Thank you," he whispers eventually.

"That's what boyfriends do."

The corners of his lips turn up the smallest bit, and I call that a win.

The rest of the drive is quiet. It's obvious Chase is still kicking himself on the inside. I just pray this new agent is who Rio says he is and will give Chase some hope.

"It's nice to meet you," a tall man greets us when we step into the apartment. "I'm Lucas. Mind if we sit?"

We move to the couches, and even though Chase smiles at the man, it's tight, so I squeeze his thigh, hoping that will set him at ease even a little bit.

"I hope you don't mind that I'm leery of agents right now," Chase tells him.

"Not at all," Lucas says. "I would be too if I were in your

shoes. I don't know the whole story, but from what little Rio did tell me, I'd say you're right to try to find a new agent. Someone should never go behind your back like he did."

"It's more than just the lying and trying to convince my boyfriend to break up with me," Chase explains. "We also found out some other shit that I can't talk about as per my lawyers' recommendations."

Lucas' eyes go wide. "Seriously?"

We both nod.

"Well, shit. Sorry for my language," he adds quickly. "I'm sorry you're going through this. I understand why you're leery of signing with another agent. I don't think I can offer anything that would put you at complete ease, but I've been given permission to give you the phone numbers of a handful of athletes I've worked with for years. You can ask them *anything* you want."

"Lucas has been amazing to me," Rio states. "And believe me when I tell you he's never done anything shady. Lucas has been my agent for almost three years now, and my dad is an accountant. If there were any fishy stuff happening behind the scenes, he would have found it."

Chase smiles at Rio. "That actually does help put some of my worries at ease," he tells his friend, then turns his attention back to Lucas. "Do you mind if I take a few days to call those contacts? It's not that I don't trust you. I just want to make sure this is the right move for me."

"Absolutely, take all the time you need," Lucas assures Chase. "And again, I'm sorry that you went through this. I have the list ready to go. I'll text it to you now." He pulls his phone out and sends Chase the list before standing. "Let me know once you've made the decision either way."

"I will. Thanks again for meeting with me," Chase says, walking Lucas to the door.

"Not a problem at all. I would love to be on your team if you think I'm the right agent for you."

Once Lucas is gone, Chase joins me on the couch again, pulling me into his arms as soon as he's seated. "Today has been a shit day," he whispers.

I kiss his chest. "It has, but we'll get through this."

"You're right because we can get through anything together." He holds me tighter and presses a kiss to the top of my head.

Damn, this man for making me all warm and gooey inside all the time. But I don't hate it.

CHAPTER TWENTY-EIGHT

MY HEART RACES as I drive with Gabe to the lawyer's office. We both had morning classes today, so we couldn't come in earlier, but Cam called me first thing this morning asking when we could set up a time to sit down with Alexander and his lawyer. Obviously, I want to put this all behind me as soon as possible, so I took it immediately when he offered a three o'clock meeting.

I was planning on calling the athletes that Lucas represents this afternoon, but that can wait until later. This is more important. I need to be free of Alexander before I can move on with my life.

"Mr. O'Callahan is waiting for you in the boardroom," a receptionist tells us and escorts us down a long hall where Cam stands by the door.

"Thanks, Sharon," he tells the lady escorting us into the boardroom.

Alexander is already waiting for us, sitting beside a stout man with greasy slicked-back hair. Neither of them appears happy to be here, but good, they shouldn't be. Alexander has been fucking stealing from me. They're lucky I didn't find out sooner, or I'd be shouting it from the rooftops, telling everyone what a piece of shit he is.

"Now that we are all here, let's start," Cam suggests, sliding a folder over to Alexander's lawyer. "Here is proof that Mr. Lee has been stealing from my client since he was hired. We aren't asking for the money to be repaid, just the severance of the contract."

Alexander's lawyer looks over the documents, then leans over to whisper to him.

"We'll agree under the condition that Mr. Anderson signs a non-disclosure agreement. He is not to talk about my client or anything that was discovered," the slimy lawyer states.

Cam looks at me, and I nod. We already knew this was going to happen.

"We accept that condition," Cam tells him.

With both parties being in agreement, Alexander and I begin signing a bunch of papers, our lawyers explaining them as we go. Once everything is settled, Alexander and his lawyer stand, shake my lawyer's hand and leave.

"You are free to sign with any agent you wish," Cam tells me with a smile.

I'm free of Alexander, but it still feels wrong that he didn't have to face any real consequences.

"How much do I owe you for all your help?" I ask, but Cam waves me off.

"It was pro-bono. You can pay me when you need someone to go over your new contract with whomever you hire."

I chuckle. "Deal."

"Are you still going to phone those athletes tonight?" Gabe asks as we head to my car.

"Yeah, I need to figure out what others have to say about Lucas because if I don't go with him, we have to find another replacement agent soon."

"I'll cook us dinner while you make the calls," he tells me.

My heart warms at his kindness. "You're the best."

His lips turn upward in an affectionate smile. "I know."

I laugh, pulling him into my arms and kissing him like he's my everything because he is.

By the time I'm off the phone with the last athlete, I feel solid in my decision. Lucas seems like a genuinely good guy. He stopped billing one of the athletes for a year when the guy's mom was diagnosed with cancer so the money could go to her treatment and wouldn't hear of the guy repaying him after she was in remission. That's the kind of person I want on my team.

"Did you make your decision?" Gabe asks.

"Lucas seems like a great guy, and after talking to a crap ton of his clients, I'm certain he's the right guy for me."

Gabe smiles. "Then make the call, baby. But make sure to send the contract to Cam before you sign."

I chuckle. "Obviously."

I take a deep breath and press Lucas' name in my contact.

"Hello?" he answers.

"Hey, Lucas, it's Chase," I reply.

"Hey, man, how are you doing?" he asks. I can hear his smile, and it puts me at ease.

"I'm doing okay. I was able to get out of my contract with Alexander today and also had some spare time to call those clients you listed," I explain.

"I'm glad to hear that. Have you decided on whether I'm the right match for you?" he checks.

"I have…" I pause for a moment and take a deep breath. "I'd love to hire you after my lawyer goes over the contract, of course."

He chuckles. "Absolutely, I'm stoked that you chose me. I think we're going to be a great match. I hope you don't mind, but I've been researching you in the hope that you would choose me," he informs me. "And your stats are out of this world."

"Thanks. I appreciate you already putting in some work.

We are going to have to contact all of my sponsors, along with the NFL, to inform them that you are my new agent. I'm not going to be an easy client for the next couple of months. I hope that's okay."

"I knew that going into this, but I'm up for the challenge," he assures me. "Text me your lawyer's email address, and I'll send over the contract to both of you shortly. Once everything is squared away, I'll have you sign a letter stating that I'm your new agent and Alexander is no longer representing you. If you can give me a list of all your sponsors, I'll ensure that gets sent to them. I should be able to send one letter to the NFL to let them know of the change, but if you know of some teams that have voiced interest in you, I'll also send a letter to them."

"I appreciate all your help," I tell him. "I'll forward all that information to you tomorrow, but I'll send my lawyer's email now."

"Thank you. I look forward to working with you," he says.

"Same," I reply and end the call.

"Everything's working out for you," Gabe says, and I smile.

"Now we just have to pray I've earned enough good karma to get signed with Michigan," I tell him and laugh.

"Even if you don't, we'll make it work out. The last week has been stressful as hell, and it didn't put a damper on our relationship at all. It gave me faith that we can make it through a year apart if we have to."

I beam at my man. "You bet your fine ass we will. You're mine, and I'm never letting you go. Nothing and no one will be able to take you away from me."

He snuggles into my chest, and I know without even being able to see his face that he's blushing.

"I love you," he whispers.

"I love you too."

CHAPTER TWENTY-NINE

Gabriel

CHASE IS PACING up and down the hall, and it's only noon. The draft doesn't start for another eight hours. He obviously didn't sleep last night since there are dark bags under his eyes, and even though he tries to hide it, he's been yawning on and off.

"You need to take a nap," I tell him, but he shakes his head.

"I'm not tired."

"And the grass is orange," I deadpan.

He pauses his pacing, staring at me with scrunched brows. "It's green. Unless something freaky is happening out there. Was it orange when you came over?" he asks, moving toward the window, but I stop him by putting my hand on his arm.

Fuck, I love this man and how obtuse he can be from time to time.

"I was using a figure of speech to call you on your bullshit," I tell him.

He sighs. "Okay, maybe I'm a little tired, but I can't sleep. I'm too anxious. When I close my eyes, all I see is the worst-case scenario..." He pauses and throws his hands up as he growls. "I'm never this nervous wreck kind of guy. I'm always calm, collected, and confident. How come today is different?" He stares intently into my eyes, begging me to have the answer, which I do.

"Because everything changes this weekend," I state in a calm, even tone. "Even if you are drafted by Michigan, life is changing for you. You'll graduate next month and will no longer be a college student-athlete. You'll be an NFL football player. That's a giant life change. Obviously, it's something you've wanted your entire life, but it's okay to be anxious. It's okay to feel like you're crawling out of your skin. This is a huge deal. It's normal for anyone to feel out of sorts in a moment like this. Let me be your rock today. You've been calming my nerves for the past few months, so let me be that person for you today. How can I help you?"

He takes a deep breath, and I step forward to wrap my arms around his middle, resting my head on his chest. His arms are quick to envelop me, and he holds me tight for a few minutes.

He yawns again, and I shake my head against his chest since he hasn't let me go. "I really think you need to rest," I voice again. "Would you like it if I laid down with you?"

"Okay," he mumbles, and I can't help but smile at his grumpiness.

Is today freaky Friday? Did we somehow switch personalities? He's supposed to be the Golden Retriever happy-go-lucky guy, and I'm the nervous grump. I don't think I'll ever be able to be all sunshine and rainbows like Chase normally is, but I can push away my nerves today and be his pillar of strength, at least for the time being.

"Come on, handsome," I say, pulling out of his arms and grabbing his hand. "Let's go cuddle."

That finally earns me the smallest uptick of his lips, but I'll take it.

In his room, I help strip him out of his clothes until he's only in his boxers, then trace my fingers over the waistband. "Do you want them on or off?" I question.

There's a strong possibility that if we lay down naked, we won't be napping, but if sex is what my man needs, who am I to say no?

"Off," he whispers, and I do as I'm told.

I pull his boxers down, and his cock is already hardening. It makes mine twitch in my pants. Suddenly, I'm torn between forcing Chase to nap and jumping his bones. Maybe sex would be a better stress reliever for him anyway. Although he'll be wired after, since he's weird like that, and for sure not wanting to sleep. *Ugh... decisions, decisions.*

"Would you like to skip the cuddling and do something more fun instead?" I ask in a husky voice while running my index finger across the length of his cock.

He moans. "Yes, please," he begs.

"Get on the bed, and I'll strip for you," I instruct, taking charge in the bedroom for the first time.

It's almost comical how fast he obeys me. I have to fight back the urge to laugh.

First, I remove my glasses and place them on his dresser, hating that everything is blurry now. With those out of the way, I slowly pull off my shirt, letting it drop to the floor beside my feet next to Chase's pile of clothes. My man is staring at me with what I think are hungry eyes. Even without my glasses, I can see the intensity in his eyes. It's like he's ready to eat me for breakfast but also enjoying the show.

I feel a little awkward as I sway back and forth, trying to act sexy while I undo the button on my jeans. I'm not sure if my dancing is turning him on or the fact that I'm opening my pants, but he licks his lips, and my cock jolts at the sight. Fuck, I want his mouth on me already.

Shoving down my need to be naked this instant, I continue to take my time and only push down my pants, leaving my underwear in place for now. Once my jeans are kicked to the side, I step toward Chase and put my foot on his knee. "Take off my socks," I command, surprised my voice doesn't wobble as my heart rate picks up.

Chase does as he's told, slipping my sock off my foot and tossing it to the floor. I switch feet, and he does the same. When both my feet are back on the floor, he moves to push my underwear down, but I shake my head.

"Patience, baby," I tell him, stepping out of his reach. "I'm in control right now, and you need to wait. You'll see my cock when I'm ready and not a moment sooner."

I had no idea being in charge like this would turn me on as much as it is, but my cock is as hard as a rock, tenting my boxers and desperate to break free.

"You're so fucking hot when you talk to me like that," Chase tells me.

His cock is leaving a trail of precum across his stomach, and it makes my mouth water.

I dance to nonexistent music, toying with the waistband of my underwear, but instead of pushing them down like I know Chase is expecting, I step forward again, kneeling in front of him.

"My mouth is watering to taste you, baby, but you have to be good and keep your hands on the edge of the bed," I tell him. He's quick to obey, so I take his cock in my hand and lick up the precum from his stomach, then the crown of his cock. I hum in appreciation of the taste. "Fuck, you're delicious."

I don't immediately swallow him down. I take my time teasing him and savoring his flavor. I swirl my tongue around the crown, lap at him from root to tip, and even suck his well-groomed balls into my mouth, which causes him to leak even more. I turn Chase into a panting, mewling mess.

Damn, he's hot like this.

"More, pleeease," he pleads.

"Do you want my mouth?" I ask, opening my lips and swallowing all of him down my throat and coming right back up again. "Or do you want my hole?" I wiggle my ass, and he throws his head back with a loud, troubled groan.

It's probably a good thing Rio isn't home because he would be giving us a hard time later. But even if he were, I couldn't bring myself to care. I love how Chase is being the vocal one for a change.

"Ass," Chase grits out, and I smile.

"Do you want to taste me and stretch me with your tongue? Or do you want me to take care of myself while I tease you with my mouth?" I question.

"Please sit on my face," he begs, wiggling with desire.

"You don't have to ask me twice."

While I slide off my boxers, Chase moves to lie in the middle of the bed. His hard cock rests against his stomach, the tip an angry red color from how hard he is, and a sticky puddle of precum is beneath it. The sight makes my mouth water again.

"Get over here and let me taste you," Chase orders, but I take my time obeying.

"I thought I was in charge?" I question with a smirk. "I didn't hear a please. Maybe I'll just stay where I am until you've found your manners."

His cock bobs from my words, and I lick my lips. It appears he likes it when I talk like this, and the heady feeling I'm getting is a high I'd love to feel from time to time.

"Please," he practically moans out. "Please let me eat your ass." His eyes are wide, begging me to give him what he wants. It's a powerful image and has my cock throbbing between my legs. I can't deny how much we both want this, but I don't rush over. I take slow, deliberate steps to prolong his anticipation.

I climb on the bed and straddle his face, leaning forward to lap up his precum.

"Finally," Chase whispers, his breath hot against my pucker.

I wiggle my ass, pressing myself down on him further, silently telling him to get on with it already, and he doesn't disappoint. His fingers dig into the globes of my ass, and he spreads my cheeks wide before diving right in.

"Yes!" I cry out, my head falling back, and I involuntarily push back on him even more, practically suffocating him with my ass.

"If I'm able to choose the way I'm going to die, it's going to be like this," he states before circling his tongue around my entrance.

It feels so good I literally get lost in the sensation. "This is my new favorite kind of cake," he tells me, then stiffens his tongue and shoves it inside me.

"Gah. Yes. Fuck. More," I whimper the words out as he eats my ass.

Wanting to give him more pleasure, I take his cock into my mouth, sucking while he stretches my needy hole. Eventually, a finger joins his tongue, followed by another and another. He isn't taking his time, getting me ready as fast as possible. It's fucking perfect because I want his cock inside me just as badly as he does.

"Grab the condoms and lube," he instructs after he's certain I'm ready.

This time, I don't scold him for not using his manners because I'm just as needy as he is. I need him inside me so bad it fucking hurts.

Once I've gotten the items, I hand the lube to Chase so he can make sure I'm nice and slick, and I rip the condom wrapper open, sliding it on his hard cock.

"How do you want me?" I ask as soon as his fingers slide out of my ass.

"I've really been loving you in charge, but I want to fuck you with everything I've got," he tells me.

I bob my head quickly. "Yes, please," I breathe out and climb off him.

"Get on all fours," he commands as he stands.

I position myself at the edge of the bed, and he grabs my hip with one hand while using the other to help guide his cock into me. A slutty mewl slips past my lips as he enters me, and Chase growls, the sound vibrating through my body, making me tingly all over.

"I don't think I'm ever going to get enough of this," he tells me, pushing his hips forward and sliding into my tight channel one inch at a time.

"So fucking good," I moan out.

Once Chase is fully inside me, he leans over my body and kisses my shoulder, neck, and ear. "What do you think about getting tested and losing the condoms?" he whispers. "I'd like to see my cum dripping out of your ass one day."

My cock twitches as the filthy image plays in my head, and I nod, unable to form words.

He stands back up, pulls his hips backward, then slams forward hard. "You're. Mine," he tells me, marking each word with a punishing thrust. "You. Belong. To. Me." His voice is husky, and his breathing is ragged as he uses my body. "And. I. Belong. To. You." Each word is punctuated with a punishing thrust, his balls slapping against me, the sound echoing with our heavy breaths.

I cry out. "Yes. Yes. Yes. I belong to you. I'm yours, and you're mine," I repeat his words back to him as he picks up his pace. His thrusts are still just as hard, but they're faster now.

Chase puts one foot on the bed so he has a better angle, and he begins to nail my prostate, causing my back to bow and tingles to form deep in my spine. If he keeps this up, I'll be coming hands-free in no time.

"Just like that," I encourage him. "Give me everything you've got."

"Fuck!" he shouts, pistoning his hips as fast as he can.

"Yes!" I yell at the top of my lungs then Chase wraps his

arm around me and grabs my cock causing me to instantly blow.

My orgasm is so strong that it makes it hard to breathe, move, or even think. Luckily, I don't have to do any of that because Chase has completely taken control.

My arms are Jell-O and refuse to keep me up anymore, so I fold them under my head. Chase's firm grip on my hips is all that keeps my legs from collapsing as well.

He continues to stroke my cock and thrust into me, chasing his release as he milks me dry. It doesn't take long before his hand stills, and he roars, filling the condom. His earlier words have me imagining what it would feel like to be bare with him, for his load to be filling my ass at this moment instead of the sheath of latex.

When Chase lets go of my hips, I collapse onto the bed, not even having the strength to move the smallest amount to miss the pile of cum, but I also don't care because one of my favorite things about sex with Chase is the way he cares for me afterward.

Chase pulls out of me and ties the condom off, throwing it in the trash can by his bed. While he does that, I shakily stand, pulling the top blanket off and tossing it to the floor to deal with later.

Chase pulls me into his arms and guides me back to the bed. "Give me a minute to feel my legs again, then we can shower."

"Sounds like a plan to me," I whisper.

My eyes are heavy like they always are after sex, and sleep quickly tries to pull me under. Oddly enough, it sounds like Chase's breathing is starting to even out too. It's not going to be fun to clean the dried cum off my stomach later, but sleep is more important right now.

As I drift off, I can't help but feel this sense of calmness wash over me. This is exactly where I'm supposed to be—in Chase's arms.

CHAPTER THIRTY

THE SOFT SOUND of Gabe's snoring wakes me, and surprisingly, I feel calm again. The anxiousness that was suffocating me earlier is mostly gone. I never fall asleep immediately after sex, but Gabe's body was the perfect distraction to pull me out of my thoughts, and shortly after, I reached the high of my orgasm, my body finally deciding to shut down for a much-needed nap. And I never sleep better than I do with Gabe in my arms.

I run my hand up and down my sexy nerd's back. He starts to shift a little, lifting his head to smile at me. "You napped," he whispers.

I nod. "You wore me out."

He beams at me and cuddles into my chest, but then he grimaces.

"There's dried cum all over me," he grumbles, and I chuckle, loving the light feeling I have once again.

"Let's clean you up then," I state, rolling over and climbing out of bed. Gabe does the same and heads straight to the bathroom.

Before I join him, I search for my phone to check the time. My family is supposed to arrive around four so we can go out for dinner before the draft starts. The shower starts as I dig through my clothes and smile when I finally find it. Thankfully, it's only three, so we have a decent amount of time to get ready.

I still can't believe I slept for almost three hours. Clearly, my body needed the rest.

"Ready?" Gabe asks from the bathroom door, leaning against it, looking all sexy.

I nod. "I'm all yours, baby," I say, waggling my brows. "And we've got an hour before my parents arrive, so we can take our time."

"I wouldn't say that," he counters. "But if you want a quickie in the shower, I'm not saying no."

I laugh and smack his ass when he turns around, his little squeak of shock causing me to laugh even harder.

I'm so glad Gabe is in my life. He centers me. I'd obviously be fine in the long run without him, but I don't want to live that life. I want him by my side forever.

My palms are sweaty as I sit on the couch with Gabe cuddled into me. My family, Lucas, Rio, and a few other friends are also in my living room, ready to watch the draft and find out if I am picked today.

Michigan isn't picking first this year, but they aren't the last ones to choose either. They are around the middle, so I just have to pray that the other teams that go before them want other players. Not all teams need a quarterback, so there is a chance they'll pass on me, and that's what I'm counting on.

"No matter what happens, we're going to get through this," Gabe reassures me.

I love how he's being my strength today when normally it's me holding him up. I guess that's what makes a healthy relationship—giving and taking and being there for the other person when they need you.

Eight o'clock hits, the draft starts, and my heart rate picks up.

We watch the television intently as the announcements start to come in. Lucas should receive a call as soon as I've been chosen, just before it's announced on television. Then, I'll probably receive a call from the owner shortly after. But that doesn't stop me from waiting with bated breath as each name gets released.

Time feels like it's going in slow motion as each team makes its selection, but before I know it, it's Michigan's turn, and my entire body goes stiff. Gabe squeezes my hand, and my dad stands behind me to clap my shoulder.

It is as if hours go by as we wait, but it's only minutes when Lucas' phone starts ringing, and everyone turns to stare at him.

"Hello?" he answers, then smiles at me. "That's great news. I'm actually here with Chase right now. I'll make sure to tell him the good news."

He says a couple more things, but I don't make it out because my ears are ringing.

Holy. Fucking. Shit. I've been chosen to play in the NFL for the team I've dreamed about playing for since I was a little kid. I don't even register the announcement coming through the television. I am in complete shock.

"Did you hear that?' Lucas asks me. I shake my head, clearing the fuzz. "You've been drafted, son. You're the newest player for Michigan."

Everyone in the room cheers, and Gabe pulls me into his arms. "You did it, baby," he whispers into my ear. "I'm so proud of you."

My phone rings a minute later, and I answer it as fast as possible. "Hello?"

"Good evening, Mr. Anderson. This is Arnold Denver, the owner of the Michigan Raptors."

I swallow the ball of nerves that has lodged itself in my throat. "It's great to hear from you, sir," I respond, my voice thankfully coming out even.

"Has your agent had a chance to speak with you?" he checks.

"Yes, sir," I tell him. "I'm so grateful that Michigan has decided to take me on."

"We're thrilled to have you. I just wanted to call you and personally congratulate you. We're looking forward to having you on our team. You're a talented young man."

"Thank you, sir," I say, expressing my gratitude. "I can't wait to go down there and meet everyone."

"We'll be in touch with more details soon, but know that everyone is excited to have you."

I thank him again, and we say our goodbyes, but it still feels surreal that this is actually happening.

"I'm a Michigan Raptor," I whisper, still clutching my phone, feeling dazed.

My dad squeezes my shoulder again. Then, this euphoric energy suddenly rushes through my body, and I jump up, pushing my fist into the air. "I'm a fucking Michigan Raptor!" I yell, and everyone cheers again, standing to give me hugs and slaps on the back.

After I'm done hugging my family and friends, I pull Gabe back into my arms and smash my lips to his, ignoring the catcalls ringing out.

My dreams are coming true right now. Not only am I playing for the team I've always wanted to, but I've got the best possible man by my side. There's nothing more a guy could ask for.

EPILOGUE

Gabriel

APPROXIMATELY EIGHTEEN MONTHS LATER

CHASE IS PRACTICALLY VIBRATING by my side as we wait for my bar exam results to be posted. I don't want to sound cocky, but I know I'm going to pass. And it's more than just being sure of how smart I am. It's also this gut feeling, which I never trusted before I met Chase. Who needs instincts when you've got brains? But Chase is kind of the opposite. He has always trusted his gut and went with the flow, believing everything happened for a reason. I'm still a facts-and-hard-work kind of guy myself, but I've also learned to accept life for what it is. Because ultimately, what will be will be, no matter how hard you work or who you pray to.

"Are the results up yet?" Chase asks, his body pressed close to mine as we sit on our couch, my laptop on my knee. I refresh the screen again, but nothing pops up.

"Not yet. You've got to be patient," I remind him.

"You know I don't do well waiting for results," he tells me, and I chuckle.

He's not wrong, but thankfully, he isn't as much of a nervous wreck as he was for the draft.

The past year has been insane with Chase playing for the Michigan Raptors and me finishing my last year of college and taking the bar exam. Life has literally gone by in a weird blur. Only recently have I felt like I'm able to breathe again.

Chase bought us a house shortly after his first season as an NFL player ended and insisted I move in with him, even though the commute was stupidly long. But I do have to admit that it is nice to spend every night in his arms, and he made the best chauffeur, so the commute wasn't boring. Those days are past us, though.

Just after I took my bar exam, Chase started training camp, preparing for his second year with the Raptors. He killed it in his first year, and he's already bringing his A-game to this new season. I couldn't be more proud of him.

Last year, I attended as many games as I could, but it was challenging to balance everything while still studying my ass off. This year is already better as I've been to every game they've played so far. I want to support my man as best as I can, and I won't be able to attend as many away games when I start working, but you best believe I won't miss a home game.

"Refresh it again," Chase insists, shoving his shoulder into mine.

I roll my eyes but do as I'm told and gasp when the results pop up.

I passed.

I fucking knew I would, but I'm still a little startled seeing the results right in front of me.

"You fucking did it!" Chase cheers and wraps his arms around me. "You're going to be the best lawyer ever."

I hug him tightly. His joy for me radiates off him and envelops me in a warm embrace.

"I'm so proud of you," he tells me, pulling back to stare into my eyes. "Now that we have the good news, you have to phone my parents, then we can celebrate." He winks, and my cheeks heat. I don't think I'm ever going to be able to stop reacting to Chase this way.

Chase doesn't wait for me to pull my phone out of my pocket, using his to call his parents. I can't help but laugh at his impatience. Though, he's probably never going to be a patient man when it comes to wanting to have sex.

The phone rings on speaker, and Hannah answers. "Did he pass?" she asks immediately.

I chuckle. "He's right here," I reply. "And yes, I passed."

Hannah squeals and pulls the phone away to shout at Oliver, telling him the good news. "We're so proud of you, honey," she tells me a moment later, and her praise brings tears to my eyes. I never heard those words from my parents. Hannah and Oliver have definitely welcomed me with open arms and have become the parents I've always wanted. They are some of the best people in the world.

"Thank you," I whisper once I find my voice again.

"We'll see you at the game on Sunday, so be prepared for extra hugs," she warns me.

My lips turn upward, and I nod even though she can't see me. "I'll be ready, but I should probably call my nana now. Thanks for being proud of me."

"Oh, honey, you don't have to thank me. That's what good parents do, and you know that we're your parents now."

"I know, but I'm still grateful to have you in my life," I tell her.

"We're lucky that Chase found you," she says, then we share quick goodbyes.

I hand Chase back his phone and pull mine out of my pocket, calling Nana next.

"You passed, didn't you?" she answers.

"I did. I'm a lawyer, Nana."

"I'm so proud of you, honey. You deserve all the good things that have happened to you more than anyone I know."

More tears prickle at my eyes, and I try to blink them away. "I couldn't have done it without you," I murmur.

"You could have, but I'm glad you didn't have to," she replies.

"Are you still coming to Chase's game on Sunday?" I check.

"Of course I am. You two have turned me into a football fan, which is weird."

I laugh. "Tell me about it. I never thought I would be a football fan, let alone dating a football player," I tell her.

"How about being engaged to one?" Chase asks, pulling a ring out of his pocket.

"Oh my God." I gasp.

"What's wrong?" Nana asks, sounding worried.

"Chase just proposed to me," I whisper, my voice catching at the end.

"Say yes and call me back later," she tells me, and the line goes dead.

"So what do you say?" he asks. "Will you marry me?"

I nod, finally letting the tears fall before launching myself into his arms. He holds me for a moment before pulling back to slide the ring onto my finger. "Now we have two things to celebrate."

I blurt out a laugh. "Take me to bed, *fiancé*."

He growls, grabs my hand, and tugs me to our room. My short legs can barely keep up, and I laugh the entire way.

If this is how the rest of our lives is going to be, I'm so game.

The End

Thank you so much for reading Schooling the Quarterback! If you loved this story please leave an honest review!

Up next is Testing the Goalie (GSU Book #2) *an m/m professor/student kinky romance.*

Imagine finding out the man you had a summer fling with is a professor at your university. He's trying to act professional but you're desperate to get his guard down and see his Daddy side again. Can you get him to agree to a friends with benefits relationship or will he continue to keep you at arm's length? Coming to Amazon and Kindle Unlimited May 9. Pre-Order Today.

ALSO BY LAURA JOHN

*** Indicates M/M romance

GSU - M/M COLLEGE SPORTS SERIES

1. Schooling the Quarterback: (An M/M Tutor/Athlete romance) ***
2. Testing the Goalie: (An M/M Professor/Student romance) ***

HUNTER SECURITY SERIES

1. Nixon: (An m/m bodyguard romance) ***
2. Denver: (An m/m best friends to lovers, single dad, bodyguard romance) ***
3. Knox: (A Suspenseful M/M Brother's Best Friend Romance) ***
4. Bennett: (An m/m bodyguard romance) ***

SULTRY SUMMER SERIES

1. Summer Heat (A FREE small town romance short story)
2. Long Summer Nights (A Small town low angst romance)
3. Summer Daze (A Small Town Interracial romance)
4. Summer Memories (A M/M second chance small town romance)***
5. Summer Dreams (A M/M Age Gap romance)***

LOVE IN SIENNA SERIES

1. Secret Smiles (A friends to lovers rock star romance) *ALSO AVAILABLE IN AUDIO!*
2. Hidden Kisses (An enemies to lovers baseball romance)

3. Guarded Hearts (A New adult, best friends to lovers, single mother romance.

4. Whispered Desires (A single mother, enemies to lovers, age gap, rock star romance)

5. Confidential Moments (A M/M Baseball romance)***

6. Clean Slates (A fast burn rock star romance)

7. Tangled Love (A rock star romance love triangle romance)

8. Restless Beat (A rock star romance)

9. Love In Sienna Boxset (Books 1-4)

10. Love in Sienna Boxset (Books 5-8)

SENTINEL PROTECTION DUOLOGY

1. Fighting Attraction (A M/M bodyguard romance)***

2. Embracing Temptation (A M/M age gap bodyguard romance)***

STANDALONES

Monster In The Shadows (Dark romance standalone)

Kissing in the snow (A M/M Christmas Novella set in the Sentinel Protection World)***

Afterglow (A kinky brother's best friend romance)

ACKNOWLEDGMENTS

Thank you so much for reading Schooling the Quarterback. I really loved writing this book and trying something new. I truly hope you love reading it!

Now onto the thank you's. There are always so many people to thank and I really hope I don't miss anyone. (But if I do I'm sorry.)

First, I want to thank my amazing team. They are everything to me and without them I wouldn't be continuing to write books. They pick me up when I feel like I'm drowning and are so much more than just personal assistants, they're friends. So give it up for the real MVPs, Brittany Franks and Suzanne Talkington!

Secondly, I want to thank my superb Alpha/Beta Readers Mandy, Robin, and Shannon. These ladies are always pointing out the beginning issues and are always available for me to bounce ideas off of. I'd probably still be stuck trying to figure things out if it wasn't for them.

Next, my sensitivity reader for making sure that Chase and Gabriel were portrayed properly. J.P Jaxson is an amazing human being that I am so lucky to call a friend and makes sure that I never miss represent the gay community. I love that he calls me out when needed and holds me to a high standard, I wouldn't want anything less.

My AMAZING editing team who helped me polish this book and make it as strong as it is today! Chantell, Lisa, Nikki, and Kaylene at Swish Designs and Editing were so amazing to work with and I don't think I am ever going to let them go.

My cover designer (who I already mentioned earlier but who also definitely deserves a second mention) Brittany Franks. Brittany is simply the best person in the entire world.

Not only is she immensely talented but she's also genuinely the most caring person I have ever met. I truly love this woman with all my heart and am NEVER letting her go.

My family for putting up with me when I put myself on a deadline and go a little crazy.

And last but obviously not least... you... the reader... without you I wouldn't be continuing to put books out! Thank you for your continued support. I love you all so much!

ABOUT THE AUTHOR

Laura is a steamy romance author from Alberta, Canada, who melds love and angst together while normalizing mental illness. She also brings a mixture of m/m and m/f books because love is love. In her books, you will fall in love with her rock stars, bodyguards, baseball players, a small town, a 2SLGBTQIA+ friendly University, and even a hired hit man!

When she's not writing, Laura enjoys reading, going to concerts, hiking, and experimenting with makeup!

If you love connecting with authors and like minded readers join Laura's Readers group!

There are a lot more books coming soon so make sure to sign up for Laura's newsletter to stay up to date on everything!